Vanishing Night

Amy Wilson

For John, with all my love.

The Turning

The moon isn't where I left it.

When I'd walked away from the pond it had still been there, and I'd thought perhaps this time the reeds would be enough to hold it in place. Somehow it must have broken free; bobbed up out of the verdant entanglement and floated away.

With the moon gone, it's going to be harder to find my way around. I make for the long shadows that will take me away from the damp, cold area of the partly frozen pond. It's Winter in this part of the garden and there's nothing living here, nothing that I have any wish to encounter anyway. There's no reason to stay.

Somewhere close by I know there will be a man, or at least something that is shaped like a man, watching me. I long to get a good look at him, to watch me the way he watches me. What is it that he sees anyway? Perhaps he had delighted in my enchantment the first time I found this place, the first time I saw the blossoms on the magnolia tree in Spring or the fiery red leaves on the acer in Autumn. But I've grown tired of moving through this place, of making my way through the turning of the seasons that never shifts, never changes, and won't release me from its spell. What does he see when he watches me now, this man who hides away in the periphery of my gaze? Is he trapped here like me, or is he the reason I'm here?

It's Summer by the topiaries and the air is warm and light. Figures cut into the hedges seem to twist and sway as I pass, and I wonder how many times I have passed this way before. Enough to remember that Summer isn't safe. Anywhere else and I might have stopped, pretended to admire the greenery, and waited to see whether the figure at my back might catch up with me, might speak to me this time - but not here. The garden is most alive in Summer, expanding so quickly that I can almost hear the plants growing, the creaking of branches like miniature hurts, like the small tears in its muscles as it strengthens them. The smell of sap hangs in the breeze, oozing from the trees like a wound. The topiaries groan as I rush past them, reaching out their branches to snag my hair, my skin.

As I dash past the last of them, I round a corner and the quality of the air changes, becomes heavier and golden-hued. The cloying scent of dying roses is everywhere. I used to love the smell of roses, but that was before. Back when I knew how to leave. My feet sink into a layer of wet leaves, musky and mildewing, and I can rest for a moment, here in Autumn where the garden takes on a calmer disposition. I turn and wait for the man but of course I can't see him. No matter which way I turn, he's only ever behind me.

I am so tired. I want to make my bed in the purple heather and rest with the garden. I don't want to drive onwards to Spring; I'm sick of being infected with its relentless hope. Last night (or was it the night before?) I'd thought that perhaps I saw a gate, but when I reached it there was nothing but the smooth obsidian of the wall, stretching endlessly into the sky. Just a trick of the light.

It's always just a trick of the light - and in Autumn I know that, but in Spring I fall for it every time.

"No more," I say, out loud, and the sound of my own voice startles me. It sounds wrong amidst the near silence of the place. The garden seems almost to shudder, and I wonder for the first time why I have not used my voice before, why I have not realised there is power in it. "I'm not playing your games anymore." I address my words to the man, or whatever he is, to the representative of this place. "Come out and face me."

There is a movement in the shadows, in the space between Autumn and Spring and I take an eager step forward before I realise that I'm being shepherded in the direction the garden wants me to take.

"Fine then. If you won't come out, I won't move on. You'll have to find your entertainment elsewhere."

The rain begins to fall then, soft at first and then a real downpour. I hold my ground while the water runs in rivulets down my face and makes rats tails out of my hair, before pooling in the mulch at my feet. I almost smile. I'm in Autumn, not Winter or even Spring, and the garden has rules. There is still a touch of warmth in the air here and there are worse things than a warm rain shower. The wind picks up, blowing through the trees and dislodging what's left of the leaves hanging there. The mournful howling seems almost to speak; as if the garden is telling me it isn't angry with my choices, just disappointed.

Still, I hold my ground. I've been walking through this garden, watching as the seasons turn, for longer than I can remember and I'm not going to do it anymore. I feel no excitement. Perhaps if I was in Spring I would have felt excitement, but here I feel only resolved, resigned to whatever happens next.

3

The wind drops. The clouds part and leave me with the clear view of the perpetual sunset. The world is moving towards evening and I catch myself yawning. I lower myself to the ground and sit amongst the heather. It's damp but so am I. What does it matter now? If I close my eyes for a moment, if I gather my strength right at the point when the garden is at its lowest ebb then maybe I'll be in with a chance of escaping.

Or is that what the garden wants me to think?

The thought blazes across my mind, but my eyelids are already heavy, the world is sliding slowly, tilting to the right as I feel cool earth under my cheek.

I feel myself start to sink into the soft ground, feel the mulch start to cover me in a slow, heavy wave. I have an impression of something slimy moving over my body, like insects, like worms and I try to scream but my mouth is filling up with loamy dirt. Maybe this is it, maybe this is the only way out of the endless turning seasons, but I don't want to do this anymore, I don't want to stay here in the ground like this.

It's only for a second and then I feel the pressure recede and I sit up and open my eyes. I stand and take a deep breath, brushing the dirt from my knees, as I look around me, frowning.

The moon isn't where I left it.

This story was first published in 3Moon Magazine's 'Growing Malcontent' Issue, in April 2021.

The Trainyard

The nights are drawing in fast as Amelia rides her bike through the streets, admiring the reflection of the diner's neon lights in the puddles as she splashes through them, sending a million miniature 'open' signs scattering across the water.

She makes it down to the crossing at the corner of West and 75th Street in record time, one fist in the air as she coasts down the hill (virtually traffic free at this time of night), inclining her head slightly to take in the imagined applause of the imagined crowd, cheering her amazing victory in the cross-town bike race.

"Thank you, thank you," Amelia says, magnanimous and grateful in her victory (but quiet in her delivery, just in case anyone from school is lurking around in earshot – she's already in danger of falling into the category of 'weird kid' and she wants to avoid that for a little while longer if she can). She's about to turn right, down 75th Street, when she pauses. She rolls up her sleeve and checks the time on her watch. Not quite half-past seven. No one will be home for a couple of hours yet, and Amelia knows she can spend a little while longer exploring the town and still be back home, in her room, doing her maths homework before her dad gets back from work. There's something in the crisp October air that speaks of adventure and Amelia smiles to herself as she turns her bike left, down West Street.

The last of the streetlights is flickering as she approaches and as she passes underneath it emits one final, sharp buzz before dying altogether, plunging the end of the street into darkness. Amelia brings her bike to a stop and fumbles around in her jacket until she finds her phone. Working with thick gloves on, she almost drops it before she shoves one of the gloves in her mouth, cringing slightly as the cold air hits her exposed fingers. She switches on the phone's torch and holds it out in front of her. The dim light isn't enough to illuminate the end of the street, but at least Amelia can see that there's nothing directly in her path. She climbs down from her bike and sets off, walking it alongside her.

"Useless town council, never fix a thing around here," she says, the words parroted from her father and muffled by the glove still hanging out of her mouth.

The shadows seem to press in from all sides, but Amelia keeps her eyes fixed on the small pool of light in front of her and keeps walking. Ten feet, five feet, two feet. Eventually she stops and lets out the breath she was hardly aware she was holding. It takes her a moment to find what she's looking for: the small space in the wire fencing. Abandoning the bike to the relative safety of the bushes, she crawls through the gap in the fence, careful to avoid snagging her jacket on the wire.

Inside the trainyard, there is dim lighting. Most of the place is abandoned, a relic of a time when the railways were new and the town was an important stop on the main transport routes, but some of the lines are still running. Amelia knows to avoid these. Her father has been careful to impress the dangers onto Amelia; the risk of getting hit by a train or of coming into contact with one of the homeless men that occasionally sleep in the yard. Amelia is mildly contemptuous of these concerns. In her world, trains always move with enough noise that you can hear them coming and homeless men are not lining up to kidnap twelve-year-old girls. Despite the dangers (or more probably, because of them), Amelia sees the trainyard as a kind of playground. She feels safe here, hidden from the world outside and free to wander the ever-changing scenery without having to explain to anyone else why she comes here, why she's so fascinated with the scent of creosote, the squeal of the wheels on the rails, or the sight of the old, partly rusted carriages.

The trains are moving tonight. Amelia can hear the low rumble coming from the far side of the yard. Making a mental note to stay away from the sound, she heads off towards her favourite place, in the deepest part of the disused section of the yard.

The lights are still working here for the most part, but they are the only thing that's still working. The train lines haven't been used in so long that they're entirely overgrown with grass and brambles, and most of them have been covered up with crates and old carriages so that they're not even visible anymore. Amelia has learned the hard way to be careful – one too many stumbles and the odd twisted ankle is a good incentive for her to memorise the safest route around the yard. Tonight, she skips nimbly between the tracks, pausing only to check whether there are any berries left amongst the thorns. She's out of luck this time; the birds have already taken anything of value.

Amelia stops in front of her favourite carriage. Most of the carriages in this part of the yard are so badly rusted that the metal has begun to flake off and fall away, but by some stroke of luck, one of the carriages in the centre of the group has been better protected from the weather. This last carriage is almost completely covered in colourful graffiti. Tonight, most of the space has been taken up by a huge sunflower motif, the yellow-orange hues bright even in the dim light. She knows that if she had come to the yard a day or two later, the scene might have changed, been painted over, and she would never have seen this. The thought that she could have missed out on something like this without even knowing about it fills her with a shaky sort of feeling, and she takes her phone from her pocket once again to snap some photos, the flash bright in the darkness. They won't hold up to the real thing, she knows, but she'll add them to her growing collection and use them to remember why it's important for her to keep coming back here in spite of all the warnings.

Amelia has never been able to catch the artist (or artists, although in her mind it's only one) at work. The closest she's ever come to it is the evening she came down straight from school to find the paint still wet on the constantly shifting canvass. Still, she dreams about one day meeting the person responsible for the art she loves so much. She dreams that they will take her under their wing and discover that she too has a talent for creating beautiful things.

She's so busy with the daydream that she doesn't hear the movement behind her until it's almost too late. She hears a wheezing, grunting sound that doesn't fit with the usual noises of the trainyard and then the unmistakable sound of footsteps. She spins, all of the excuses for her presence flying from her mind as she turns. But it's not a yard worker or a security guard, or – worst of all – her father. It's a man, stooped and shuffling awkwardly towards her, his torn jeans rippling in the cold wind.

"Are you alright?" she asks, frowning.

The figure makes that strange wheezing, grunting sound again and this time there is something else too, the smell of something spoiled and rotten spilling forth from inside his mouth. It hits Amelia so hard that it makes her nose sting and her eyes water. She takes a step back, covering her nose with one hand.

The figure carries on moving, neither faster nor slower than before, and as it does so, it moves directly under one of the lights.

Now Amelia can see the pallor of its skin, can see the way it seems to hang loosely from its bones as if it doesn't quite belong there. Worse still, she can see how the man can't manage to fully close his mouth over rows and rows of pointed teeth. She backs up until she's touching the sunflowers, until the cold, hard metal is pressed against her back. Her phone falls from her numb fingers and she takes a half-step towards it just as the thing lurches for her. Amelia throws herself to the ground, rolls under the carriage and draws her knees up into her chest, folding herself up, making herself as small as she can. She hardly dares to breathe.

She can see the figure pacing around the carriage, can see where the sole of its boots are coming apart, its dirty skin showing underneath. For a moment, she allows herself to hope that perhaps the creature's clumsy gait won't allow it to crouch down and follow her, but then she feels the carriage start to move. It rocks backwards and forwards and then – as Amelia lets out a despairing scream – it topples entirely, crashing into one of the other carriages. She scrambles out from underneath it and is back on her feet just in time to see it fall - the sunflowers vanishing into the dirt.

The creature stands in the jagged ruins of the broken mess, blocking her path back to the street. Amelia could swear it's trying to pull its sagging features into a grin. Without thinking about where she's going or how she's going to get out, she turns and runs.

9

She almost falls twice before she even makes it into the main part of the yard; once when she catches her foot on a hidden piece of track and once when she runs through some brambles. Each time she barely keeps her footing, each time she imagines the creature getting closer to her if she slows.

The sound of the trains is louder here, and she realises that she's made it to the part of the yard she normally avoids, the part populated by workers. She doesn't know her way around and she hesitates for a second. And in that second, a hand descends on her shoulder.

Amelia screams and tried to twist away, but she can't get free. She kicks out in a blind panic and makes contact with something solid.

"Hey!" a voice shouts.

A human voice.

She forces herself to stop struggling and looks up into the face of a large man in a security guard's uniform. Amelia thinks she recognises him, she's hidden from him more than once.

"You're not supposed to be in here," he begins.

"Please," she interrupts, her voice strained and high-pitched. "He's chasing me!"

"Who is?" He follows her gaze.

The man is still coming for her. He's still moving in that slow, shambling way but, despite the fact that he doesn't appear to be moving any faster than he was, he's almost caught up to her. He's no more than ten feet away.

"Right." The guard lets her go, takes a heavy torch from his belt. "I'll deal with this."

"Wait." It's her turn to clutch at him. "Please, he's dangerous. I think he's ... I think he's not human."

She hears how it sounds. She knows even as she says it that it won't be enough to convince him. To save him.

"Please," she says again.

He shakes his head at her and turns away. Torch raised, he advances on the man. Amelia can't hear what he says next, she can only watch as he recoils, as he swings the torch in the creature's direction.

The thing moves faster than she could've imagined. It dodges the guard's attack and lunges at him, grabbing him around the neck and opening its mouth wide. There is a terrible wet, tearing sound and then the guard slumps to the ground. Amelia can't see what's happened to him. A small, guilt-ridden part of her is grateful for that.

The creature looks up and there's something wet and shiny on its face now, something that Amelia doesn't want to look at. It's making a different sort of noise now, a kind of choking sound as if it has something stuck in its gullet. And then, before she has time to react, it moves towards her and she can see how it managed to catch up to her before, because the thing isn't slow at all, it's fast, maybe even faster than she is and she doesn't know how to get away.

Out of the corner of her eye, she notices something moving. She hears the squeal of metal against metal, feels the rumble of the heavy train moving, and remembers where she is. In a flash, Amelia knows exactly what she's going to do: she's going to break every promise she's ever made to her father.

Without giving herself time to think, she sprints for the tracks. One wrong move, one foot snarled on brambles, one small stumble and Amelia knows she's dead. She can hear the thing moving behind her, hear the wet, gurgling noise emanating from its throat, hear the slap of its partially booted feet as they strike the ground. And now, she can see the train, the lights blindingly bright against the October evening. Breathing hard, forcing cold air into her lungs, she waits until the very last second when the train is almost upon her, and then, she leaps.

The pain in her arm in incredible. There's a moment where she isn't sure whether she made it, whether the train ploughed into her as she crossed in front of it. But then she opens her eyes and realises she's lying on the ground next to the tracks. The creature is gone, one torn and bloody boot lying on the track the only sign that it was ever there. In the distance, she can hear the scream of the engine's breaks mingled with the sound of men shouting.

Using her good arm, she pushes herself to her feet and sets off back through the yard. She can't look at the place where the graffitied carriage used to be; she keeps her eyes averted as she passes. She tells herself that there will be time to think about that later, for now she just has to get home. There's a moment, when she's crawling through the hole in the fence where she feels something catch at her jacket and she screams before she realises that she's only snagged it on one of the sharp pieces of wire. She pulls herself free, ripping the back of the jacket in the process, exposing more of herself to the cold night air. She hardly notices.

It takes two attempts for her to pick up the bike, working one-handed. Balancing it against her side, she sets off slowly down the street. As she gets to the corner at the crossroads, the street light closest to the yard flickers back into life. Amelia doesn't turn around.

She doesn't see the man in torn dungarees, shambling down the street.

The Rollercoaster

He'd known as soon as he saw her that she would be afraid to ride. It was the expression on her face, a wide-eyed, searching stare that took in the people in the queue, the signs, and finally, him.

He caught her eye and she tried to smile, but it came out weak and watery. He was about to smile back (he'd learned enough over the years to manage a half-decent impersonation of reassurance), when a little girl near the front of the queue turned to her mother and said, "Mummy, can we ride the horses again?"

"Again?" her mother asked, stressing the second syllable in the mock-surprised tone of parents everywhere. "Would you mind?" she asked, turning to him, and he said, "Of course not."

He opened the little gate behind him, the one with the sign that read, 'exit'.

"Have fun," he said to the girl as she passed.

The child waved happily and, the mother gave him a grateful smile. The small crowd watched as they vanished in the direction of the carousel. Most of them were silent, a few smiled indulgently, and one woman looked as though she might be trying to hold back tears.

The queue moved forward again and the young woman with the wide-eyed stare and the watery smile was almost at the front. This time he did manage to smile at her.

She responded by fixing her gaze on the ground.

He let the next few people pass, taking a token from them before he let them through the turnstile, and making sure that they were securely in the carriage before he sent the ride on its way.

"Next," he said, looking at the girl.

She froze.

A man in line behind her moved forward without looking, bumping into her. A couple of people started to mutter.

He gestured to them to go around the girl. "It's okay," he said to her. "You can stand here with me. People can get past."

Her eyes flicked to the 'exit' sign and then back to his face. For a moment, he thought that she might bolt for the gate.

"It's okay," he said again. Coaxing, as if he was talking to a small child or an injured pet.

She nodded and left the queue, squeezing in next to him, careful not to touch him or to touch the ride controls.

For several long minutes they stood together in silence as people filed past. Young and old, couples and singles, parents and children, he performed the same ritual with each of them, taking their token, checking their restraints and waving, once, before he started the ride.

"Could I leave?" She indicated the exit gate.

He considered. "Have you done everything you wanted to do?"

"Yes." She blinked, as if surprised by her own answer.

"Been on all the other rides, eaten too much popcorn, lost at all the carnival games?"

This time she laughed. "Yes, all of that. It's been a nice evening, actually."

"Then you might as well stay," he said. "You'll only end up back here anyway."

She regarded him with something like curiosity. "What about you? Have you been on any of the rides or played any of the games?"

"Me?" He was taken aback. He wondered whether anyone else had ever asked him that question and came to the conclusion that they probably hadn't. He would have remembered. "No, I don't get to go on any of the rides. I just do this." He gestured at the controls.

She didn't look surprised. "That's a shame," she said. "The waltzers are good here."

He stored the information away in the back of his mind. He doubted whether he would ever experience the waltzers himself, but perhaps, he thought, it could be a talking point with his next nervous customer.

"Maybe I'll try them one day," he said. "Thank you." He indicated the rollercoaster. "What do you think then? Are you ready?"

"I'm not sure," she said. "It looks like a big drop."

"I've heard it's fun."

She squinted at the track, as if she was trying to see around the bend. "Do you think it goes upside down?"

He followed her gaze. "It might do."

"I'm still not sure. Is it okay if I stay here a while longer?"

He nodded. "Take your time."

Ahead of them, people cheered and whooped as the ride began. She watched them until they vanished behind the curve. To their right, an empty cart pulled up slowly.

"Do you think it's silly?" she asked.

"To be afraid? Of course not. I think everyone is afraid, if they're being honest about it."

She bit her lip. "They all seem so excited about it. I wish I had someone to ride with."

She looked so hopeful that he felt his heart stir for her, but he shook his head, nevertheless. "I can't. It's against the rules."

She nodded and looked away from him, out towards the edge of the funfair where the sun was dipping into a perpetual sunset. "Have you been here long?" she asked.

"Forever."

"And have I been here long?"

"Longer than some," he admitted.

She took a deep breath. "I think I'm ready."

He smiled and held out his hand. She placed a small, silver token on his palm, and he let her through the turnstile.

She settled herself into the carriage, pulled the safety bar down over her lap, and raised her hand to him in a small, uncertain wave. She mouthed something at him that he thought might have been 'goodbye'.

As the ride jolted into life, he kept his eyes fixed on her face, watching as her expression moved from fear to determination to something like relief. He kept his eyes on her face and deliberately ignored the small, stylised logo on the side of the carriage. The one that read 'Styx'.

Vanishing Night

"Don't let your children out of your sight. Beware! Beware! It's Vanishing Night!"

Cassie watched the younger children as they spun in circles, their eyes hidden behind their hands, as they chanted. She wished that they would play something else, but she understood. 'Vanishing Night' had been her favourite game once as well.

The children were still spinning when one of the women from the village came to break up the game. She had a long nose and striking green eyes, and the air of someone who spent every spare minute working.

"That's enough of your nonsense," she said, grabbing a boy and a girl by the hands and dragging them away. "And on tonight of all nights."

Cassie recognised the children as Ivy and Harry. They were around her brother's age, and they came by the farm often. They had the same features as their mother – the same green eyes. There was no mistaking the family resemblance.

She shook her head as she watched the woman lead them away, still scolding them. Cassie wondered whether the woman had ever played the game herself, when she had been a child. She'd noticed that people tended to forget the things that brought comfort to children, as they grew older.

"Cassie." Her mother's voice broke into her thoughts. "Are you all done?"

Cassie stood, brushing dried grass from her skirts. "All done," she said.

"Fed the chickens? Seen to the calf?" Her mother hesitated. "Packed your bag?" she added after a moment.

"Yes," said Cassie. She thought about how like her mother it was to nag her about her chores – even tonight. Even when she might not be here in the morning. She tried to put the thought out of her mind.

"Where's Toby?" she asked her mother.

"At the house having something to eat. Which is where we should be." Her mother held her hand out – an uncharacteristic gesture. "Come on," she said, giving Cassie's fingers a light squeeze. "It's going to be a long night."

Back at the house, Cassie checked Toby's bag. As she'd expected, he had packed three stuffed bears and no warm clothes. She re-packed it for him while he peppered their mother with questions.

"Why are we all sleeping in the church?"

"We just thought it might be a nice thing to do," their mother answered. "It'll be fun. Like being at a party."

Toby frowned. "Is it because of Vanishing Night? Are any of the children going to vanish?" His eyes filled with tears. "Am I going to vanish?"

"No," Cassie said fiercely. She shoved one of the stuffed bears back into the bag and fastened it closed. "You're not going to vanish. I'm going to look after you."

"Promise?" Toby sniffed.

"We're all going to look after each other," their mother said. "And we'll all come home safe tomorrow morning, you'll see."

Her eyes met Cassie's over the top of Toby's tousled curls. They were full of doubt.

There wasn't much space to lie down in the church. The pews had been moved against one wall and were piled on top of each other in a way that seemed precarious to Cassie, but even though this had created more floor space, with the whole village plus their bags all in one place it felt cramped and claustrophobic.

Cassie sighed. Her mother had been right, she realised. It was going to be a long night. She shifted, trying to find a position where her shoulder-blades didn't feel like they were trying to dig a hole through the stone floor. Finally, she admitted defeat and sat up.

Her mother was dozing, her back against the wall and one arm wrapped around Toby.

All around them, people lay still or sat in small groups talking quietly. None of the children moved. Most of them, like Toby, were huddled against their parents.

With her mother asleep, Cassie took the opportunity to stretch her legs. She crept carefully to the doors, picking her way between sleeping bodies.

One of the burly men standing guard nodded to her.

"Now then, young Cassie," he said. "This must be your second time, surely?"

She shook her head. "I'm fourteen," she said. "I was born just after..."

"Just after the last time," he finished softly. "Born in a vanishing year. Your poor mother."

He looked so sad that for a moment she wondered whether he might have lost somebody.

"Nothing to worry about," he said, collecting himself with a visible effort. "Me and Emmett will make sure that nothing goes in or out of this door until sunrise, won't we, Emmett?"

The other man let out a grunt that Cassie assumed was an affirmative.

She wanted to ask whether they really believed what they were telling her, whether they really thought that huddling together inside the church would keep them safe, but she stayed silent. She already knew the answer – in over ten generations, no one had yet found a way to protect all of the children of the village on this night. There were no better plans.

"Go on back to bed," the man said.

Cassie nodded and was about to bid him goodnight when a breeze blew in under the door, carrying with it a cloud of dust. She blinked the dust from her eyes, and when she opened them again, the man had gone.

Cassie whirled. Everyone had gone.

And then she heard it – the sound of a child crying. She raced back to where she had left her family and found Toby, still asleep, the stuffed bear pressed against his cheek. Cassie grabbed him and held him close.

He awoke with a squeal of protest.

Around them, other children were beginning to wake. Some cried out for their parents, others stood, stock-still and staring, and some joined in the wordless bawling.

Gods, thought Cassie. *It's just us. All of the adults have gone.*

"Cassie?" Toby was pulling at her sleeve. "What's happening? Where is everyone?"

"Come on," she said, helping him to his feet. "Follow me."

She walked to the centre of the church. "I need everybody to listen to me," she said. Her voice sounded strange in her ears – as if it was coming from a long way away – but her words came out clearly. "I need you all to come here so that I can check we're all still here."

Harry shuffled forward, still wailing, and Cassie realised he had been the one she heard cry out.

She knelt down so that her face was level with his. "I need you to stop crying now, Harry. It's going to be alright."

The boy didn't stop altogether, but his wails did soften into quiet sobs.

Good enough, Cassie decided.

The other children gathered around, and Cassie made them stand still so that she could count them. Eleven including herself. She sent up a brief prayer of thanks that there were no babies among them.

"Everyone put your warm clothes on and then come straight back here," she said.

"Why do we need our warm clothes? We're not supposed to leave the church." Ivy said.

Cassie hesitated. She didn't want to tell the gathered children that everything was different now – that she had no idea what was going to happen next. Instead, she said, "There aren't as many people here now. The church will be colder. We should all wrap up."

She was helping Toby into a woollen jumper when he said, "Cas-sie", splitting her name into two distinct and frightened-sounding syllables.

She turned to find that a light was forming over the altar.

"What is it?" breathed one of the girls. "Is it an angel?"

The light resolved itself into the shape of a figure, dressed in a brilliant white robe. It let out an unholy shriek and dived, heading for the children.

"Run!" Cassie yelled. "Don't let it touch you!"

The children scattered, hiding behind pillars and diving under pews.

One of the older boys headed for the door, and then stopped, uncertainty clouding his features.

"Get them open," Cassie shouted at him.

He nodded to her and heaved at the door, using his whole weight to push it open.

26

"Outside," Cassie said, giving Toby a little push. "Go."

She followed him, letting out a breath as she saw the children gathered on the path.

"Let's get this door shut," she said, putting her shoulder against it and beginning to push.

"Wait!" Harry screamed. "Ivy is still in there!"

Cassie peered inside and swore. The girl was still hiding under the pew, her eyes wide and full of fear as she looked out at them.

Cassie beckoned to her, but Ivy shook her head.

She tried again, more urgently this time, and the girl crawled a few inches forward.

And the white-robed figure descended.

Ivy threw herself backwards, screaming.

From outside, Cassie could see that Ivy had managed to dodge the creature's grip, but she was trapped under the pew with no way to make it to the door.

"Stay here," she told Toby and – before he could protest – she ran back into the church.

Keeping to the wall, she made her way to the right of the figure. She moved quietly, but it seemed pre-occupied with trying to prise Ivy from her hiding-place and if it was aware of Cassie's presence, it didn't react.

"Hey," she yelled. "Over here."

The thing turned. Cassie got an impression of a face beneath the hood – all sharp angles and sharper teeth – and then it let out a shriek and flew towards her.

"Run, Ivy," Cassie yelled, taking off towards the back of the church. She didn't have time to check whether the girl had done as she was told. She raced towards the back wall, drawing the creature along with her, and ducked behind the altar. There was no time for her to catch her breath – she could hear the thing behind her. Cassie used her momentum to propel her around the altar and back towards the doors. She felt an icy wind pass over her head and for a moment she thought the thing had her, but then she ducked, and it swooped away. She re-doubled her efforts and made it to the doors just ahead of the creature.

The other children were already standing ready to push the doors closed. Cassie ran the last few steps, turned, and half fell against the doors as she helped to close them.

She expected to hear the sound of something heavy slamming into the doors from the outside, and she braced herself against it.

There was nothing.

Toby was crying. "You scared me," he said.

She bent and wrapped him in a hug. "I scared me a little bit too," she admitted. She gave him one last squeeze and turned to Ivy. "Are you hurt?"

Ivy shook her head, her face pale.

"Did it touch you?"

"No."

Cassie let out a breath. "Good. That's good." She turned to the others. "I don't think we should stay here."

"Will that thing stay trapped in the church?" one of the boys asked.

"I hope so."

"Where do we go?" he asked.

"I want to go home," Toby said.

Cassie considered. The sun lay low on the horizon, not much more than a vague blur of pinkish light, as if dawn was just about to break. It was gloomy but light enough to see.

"Come on," she said. "We'll try everybody's houses one by one. Stay together."

She took Toby and Harry by the hands and let Ivy hold onto her sleeve.

"Cassie?" Ivy asked in a whisper. "What happens if it touches you?"

Cassie tried not to shiver. "I just don't think it would be a good idea," she said.

They searched the houses one by one, starting with the ones closest to the church and ending with the ones on the outskirts of the village, near to the fields. They were all empty.

"Where is everybody?" Toby asked. His voice had a strained quality to it that Cassie knew meant more tears were coming.

"It'll be alright," she said. "It's going to be light soon and then -" she broke off.

They had been searching through the village for almost an hour, she realised. In that time the sun had not moved. The clouds had not moved. Cassie stared at the bright spot on the horizon - and it was like looking at a painting.

"And then?" Toby prompted.

"Hmm? Oh, and then I'm sure everything will be alright."

He frowned and looked as though he was going to say something else, but before he could speak, Ivy let out a small cry.

They all turned and followed her gaze. A streak of white light was coming towards them, moving quickly.

"Run!" Cassie shouted. "Get to the fields."

The children ran down the path and scrambled over the fence, the older children lifting the younger ones over it.

"Spread out," Cassie told them. "Hide."

They headed for the cornfields and ran between the tall stalks.

Cassie held tight to Toby's hand, but she lost sight of the other children as they scattered.

"Did it get out of the church?" Toby panted. "Or are there two of them?"

The figure flew by overhead, so close that the tops of the plants moved, and again Cassie felt the sensation of biting cold as it passed.

She put a finger to her lips and Toby nodded, covering his mouth with his hand as if to keep his voice from leaking out.

The stalks a few feet away wobbled, as if something was moving amongst them.

Cassie positioned herself in front of Toby and motioned to him to move away. They both backed off slowly, trying to avoid disturbing the plants as much as possible.

The movement stopped. Cassie was about to tell Toby to hurry when Harry appeared. The boy flinched when he saw them, and Cassie raised her hand in warning. He nodded and took several deep breaths.

"Did you see it?" Cassie whispered.

Harry shook his head.

"Where are the others?"

"We got split up."

"Stay close. We'll find them."

They moved quietly through the field for several long minutes. Once, Cassie thought she heard a scream, but she couldn't tell where it was coming from – or even whether it was human. She swallowed hard, praying that the other children were all safe.

They must have lost their bearings because, when the little group pushed forwards, they abruptly found themselves standing in the open.

"Is it gone?" asked Harry, but Cassie wasn't listening.

She was staring at the sun. "It moved," she whispered, almost to herself. "It's moving."

She was about to tell the others the good news – that dawn would be here soon – when she heard a screech overhead. She looked up, just as the hooded figure dived at them.

The three children ran back into the cornfield.

The creature followed. It didn't bother trying to keep quiet – it didn't even bother trying to dodge the tall plants, instead, it ripped through them, uprooting and then discarding them behind it.

Cassie could feel the thing gaining on them, could feel the chill of it, like ice water on the back of her neck.

"Split up," she yelled.

Toby and Harry ran in opposite directions.

Cassie stopped and faced the creature. All the fight seemed to drain out of her, and she felt her whole body go cold.

The creature moved forwards, slower now, and as it did so it reached towards her.

Cassie saw a pale, skinny hand emerge from under its robe. She sank to her knees, her breaths coming in short puffs that were visible in the freezing air.

The figure's hand moved closer, almost close enough to touch her face.

Cassie shut her eyes.

"Cassie!" She heard Toby's shout and she forced her eyes back open.

Somehow, Toby had found Harry, Ivy and one of the other children, and the four of them were standing behind the creature, staring.

The creature's head whipped round, and it let out a sound that was half-way between a hiss and a growl.

"Toby, no," Cassie managed to croak out. "Run."

She tried to push herself up, but her body felt as if it was encased in ice, and she fell, shuddering, back to her knees.

The figure moved towards the group of children, one arm outstretched, and Cassie could only watch as it inched closer to them. She felt tears running down her face and she offered up one last silent prayer to any golds that might be listening.

And at that exact moment, the sun finally rose high enough in the sky for its rays to fall over the cornfield.

The creature looked up and let out a sound like a wounded animal. It took a step backwards, and then another, one arm raised to shield its face from the light. Finally, with an anguished shriek, it flew up from the ground and vanished into the rapidly warming morning air.

Cassie eased herself to her feet, just as Toby threw himself at her, almost knocking her back down again.

"It's alright," she told him, patting him on the back. "We're alright."

"Is it gone?" Ivy asked.

Cassie nodded. "The sun's almost up." She pointed to the place in the sky where a pale pink light was growing stronger. "I think we're safe now." She turned and shouted into the field. "You can come out now."

"Come out!" shouted Harry.

"The monster's gone," added Ivy.

It took some time for them to coax out the rest of the children, and by the time they did so they could already hear the church bells ringing.

"That's our parents. They'll be looking for us," Cassie said. "Quick, back to the church."

They raced back through the village. As Cassie had said, their parents were standing outside, calling their names.

The sky was almost completely pink when Cassie spotted her mother, standing in the crowd, an anxious expression on her face.

"Mother!" Toby yelled, letting go of Cassie's hand as he flung himself into their mother's arms.

"I was so worried." Their mother grabbed Toby and held him tightly. "We looked everywhere, but we couldn't find you." She looked up, frowning. "Where's Cassie?"

"I'm here," Cassie said. She tried to put a hand on her mother's shoulder, but it passed right through her, as if her flesh was made out of mist.

"Toby? Where's your sister?"

Toby looked behind him and for a moment, Cassie thought he was looking at her. Then he frowned and she realised he was looking right through her.

"She was just here," he said, a tremble in his voice.

Cassie was about to start shouting and waving her arms – to *make* them see her – when she spotted the figure in white. It was standing near to Harry and Ivy.

In her rage, Cassie forgot to be afraid. She marched up to the figure.

"You can't have them," she said. "Vanishing Night is over and they're safe. Leave them be."

The figure pushed back its hood, revealing the face of a girl only a little older than Cassie. A girl with a long nose and striking green eyes. There could be no doubting the family resemblance.

"You're their sister," Cassie said.

The girl nodded.

The soft, pink glow in the sky began to grow until it filled the air around them.

The figure held out her hand to Cassie.

Cassie took hold of it. The girl's fingers were as cold as ice. As cold as death.

As they stepped forward together, Cassie turned and took one last look at Toby.

"I'll come back for you," she whispered.

The moon had already risen by the time the coach pulled up in front of the house.

Diane pushed aside the curtain and took her first tentative look at the place. She let out a sigh of relief. In her darker hours she had imagined that she might be spending her apprenticeship in a house that resembled that of a witch's castle from a fairy-tale – all sharp angles and crumbling towers – but even in the semi-darkness, the house looked reassuringly ordinary.

It stood, perched at the end of a stone path and neatly flanked by hedges on either side. The front door stood open, and a pool of warm and welcoming light spilled out.

Diane opened the door and jumped down.

The coachman was already unloading her bags. He carried them into the house, and nodded at the occupant and then at Diane, before he departed, leaving them staring at each other.

"Well," said the Perfumier. "Let me look at you."

She raised her lantern and scrutinised Diane's face.

Diane regarded the woman in return. She was small and neat, dressed in a dark smock and apron. Her greying hair was pulled back into a severe bun, but she had wrinkles around her eyes that suggested that she smiled honestly and often.

The woman seemed satisfied with Diane, because she gave her arm a little squeeze, smiled, and said, "You must be tired. I'll show you to your room."

The house was dark, and Diane was glad to follow the Perfumier as she strode through the corridors with her lamp. When they reached the apprentice's room, there was a fire in the grate, although it had long since burned down to embers. The room was simple, containing only a bed, a set of drawers and an old trunk pushed against the wall.

"This is lovely," Diane said. "Thank you."

The Perfumier accepted the compliment without comment.

"Here," she said, reaching into her apron and drawing out a small bottle.

"You made this for me?" Diane took it between her fingers as if she was afraid she might crush it.

"What do you smell?"

Diane unstoppered the bottle and held it under her nose, her eyes closed as she inhaled.

"Roses," she said. "And something fruity." She opened her eyes. "I'm sorry I -"

The Perfumier held up her hand. "We all begin somewhere," she said. "Get some rest. It is my custom to rise early, and I will expect you to be available when I want you."

"Yes, Ma'am. Thank you for the perfume."

"Keep it with you," the woman said, as she closed the door, leaving Diane to undress by the light of the dying fire.

The Perfumier was true to her word. She rose just after first light each day - and she kept Diane busy fetching water, scrubbing the floors, and moving stacks of books and papers from the little library to the table in the workroom and back again.

"You are not to enter the workroom for any other reason," she told Diane. "And you are not to enter the kitchen at all."

"But then how am I going to help you make perfume?"

The woman gave her a long look.

"What does your perfume smell like?" she asked.

Diane frowned. "Roses and fruit," she said.

The Perfumier was silent for a moment. "For now, you may help me by sweeping the path outside the house," she said, taking a book from the top of the pile and beginning to flip through its pages.

They fell into a daily routine. The Perfumier would assign Diane some cleaning tasks, before vanishing into the kitchen to work. Several times each day she would emerge to ask Diane about the perfume, and each time she would listen to Diane's answer, nod, and then return to the kitchen.

Diane spent so much time sniffing the little bottle of perfume that she began to fear she would lose the ability to smell it altogether - that it would disappear into the background scents of her life, like the smell of the ink in the workroom or the smell of lye as she scrubbed the floors for what felt like the hundredth time. She took to putting a tiny tab of the scent on her pillow before she lay down for the night – as if hoping that her dreaming mind might be able to unlock what her conscious mind could not.

And sure enough, there came a morning when she opened her eyes, and smiled. She had it!

"Blackberry," Diane said, as the Perfumier entered the morning room. "The fruit in the perfume is blackberry."

The woman smiled. "Very good," she said. "Now tell me what you can smell."

Diane's own smile faltered. "But I just told you."

"No, you told me the ingredients. I asked you to tell me what you can smell."

The woman crossed the room and eased Diane into a chair. She sat opposite her and regarded the girl calmly.

"Close your eyes," she said. "Tell me where the scent takes you."

Diane closed her eyes and breathed deeply. Nothing happened for several, long moments, and she was about to tell the Perfumier that it was no good, that the scent hadn't taken her anywhere, that perhaps she just wasn't suited to the work after all, when a rush of images flooded her mind.

She was a child of eight or nine years old again, and it was the summer that she and her sister had stayed with their aunt in the country. Left to their own devices, they had spent the days exploring, climbing trees, building dens by the river, and picking wild roses to plait into each other's hair. When the blackberries had ripened they had picked their way through the thorns to grab handfuls of them. They had gorged themselves on the riverbank that afternoon, as they lay back and watched the fish leap, watched the light play on the surface of the water, and it had felt to Diane like a kind of magic. But it was a magic tinged with sadness – the blackberries heralded the changing of the seasons and the end of their summer adventures.

Diane opened her eyes and stared at the Perfumier, lost for words.

The woman smiled again, the skin at the corners of her eyes crinkling.

"Eat your breakfast," she said, pushing a bowl towards Diane. "This morning I will show you the kitchen."

Diane's duties changed. In the mornings she would gather herbs and flowers from the garden, or go to town to buy groceries. In the afternoon she would help the Perfumier with her work. Diane would be expected to take notes and to pass ingredients and equipment to the Perfumier when she asked for them. She learned to be quick and to anticipate the woman's needs, for she had a sharp tongue when she felt that Diane was being too slow. If they didn't have a commission, Diane would retire to her room, poring over heavy tomes with titles like 'Scent and the Evocation of Memory'. Sometimes, new clients would come, and she would be allowed to stay in the small sitting room that doubled as a consultation room, as long as she remained quiet.

Many of the clients were young women, brides-to-be who wanted something special for their wedding day. Or for their wedding night.

"These women are our bread and butter," the Perfumier told Diane, as she poured liquid from a sunshine-coloured bottle into the pot. "Come here and tell me what you smell."

Diane breathed deeply. "Hope," she said.

The woman smiled.

The Perfumier was with a new client when the bride-to-be came back for her perfume. Diane fetched it, accepting both the money and the young woman's effusive praise with a smile and a slight blush. As she escorted the woman to the door, however, Diane couldn't help but notice how she stared at the dusty skirting boards, how she pursed her lips and wrinkled her nose at the state of the floor tiles.

"Am I still supposed to be cleaning?" Diane asked the Perfumier when she returned to the workroom. "It's just that I've been busy, but the house is a bit messy and one of the clients -"

"Hmm?" The woman seemed distracted. "What? Cleaning? No, you're far too busy to bother with that. Go and hire one of the girls in town to do it."

"Which girl?"

"Any. Find one that smells of drudgery and offer her a copper coin a week to come here."

Diane's mouth dropped open, but the Perfumier ignored it.

"Be quick about it. We have a new commission, and I will require your help with it." She brushed past Diane and headed to her desk, muttering.

"A copper coin a week," Diane said, her tone almost pleading.

The straw-haired girl she was speaking to regarded her without a word for a moment, and then she turned and spat deliberately on the ground next to Diane's shoe.

"It's a fair price," Diane said.

"It would be a fair price for anyone else," said the girl. "But not for the witch."

"She isn't a witch," Diane said. "She makes perfume."

"Aye, from the ground-up bones of babies." The girl spat again.

"I live there. I've seen what she does. It's all herbs and flowers. No dead babies, I promise." Diane made a crossing motion across her chest.

The girl glared at her, and then her expression changed to something more calculating. "I'll not stay after dark," she said.

"You won't have to," Diane promised.

"And I'll take the coin from you, not from her."

"Alright."

"Alright then." The girl stuck out her hand and Diane took it, relieved she hadn't spit into her palm. "I'll come tomorrow."

"Thank you," Diane said.

As she was leaving, the girl said, "She's an unfeeling creature. You're mad to stay with her."

She turned back to argue, but the girl was already walking away.

The new client was a man – the first, the Perfumier told Diane, that they had acquired in a long time.

"His wife died recently, and he wants something to help him remember her," she said.

They worked on the scent for weeks. Three times, the Perfumier burst into Diane's room in the night to bid her to gather a new ingredient or to help with a new concoction. Twice, she made them throw away the entire batch and start again.

Finally though, it was ready. Diane sat in the consultation room and watched as the old man opened the bottle.

The scent drifted around the room. In it, Diane could pick up the tang of sea-salt and long walks across darkened winter beaches, the dusty smell of old books and long evenings spent in companiable silence in front of the fire. When she came back to her senses, she realised that her face was wet with tears.

The old man too was crying. "Thank you," he said, pressing the Perfumier's small hands between his own. "Thank you for bringing her back to me."

The Perfumier helped him to the door, offering her arm for him to lean on. When he was gone, she turned, dry-eyed, to Diane.

"You should not cry in front of clients," she said.

There were dark rumours flying around the town.

A sickness had taken all of the children in one family, almost overnight, and there were protective talismans hanging from every door frame as Diane passed.

The shopkeeper still sold food to her, but he no longer smiled or asked her any questions, and he made sure that their fingers didn't brush against each other as he passed her the groceries.

The cleaning girl stopped coming, and Diane did not try to engage another.

She had just finished scrubbing the floors and was heading out into the garden to collect mint, when the boy came to the house. It was not a common occurrence to have a boy at the house, but she usually wouldn't have thought much about it. After all, he could be delivering a message or picking up a package for a client – there were any number of legitimate reasons for his presence. But there was something about him – something about the expression on his face as he passed Diane on the path. It was predatory, almost wolf-like.

45

She shivered in the cool morning air and, despite taking only a few minutes to fill her basket, she did not return to the house until she was sure he would have had enough time to conduct his business and leave.

The house was quiet when she entered it. Diane listened at the consulting room door for a moment, but when she heard nothing, she let out a breath and made her way to the kitchen to take the herbs for drying.

A small doll lay just outside the door, face down, as if it had been accidentally discarded. Diane picked it up and turned it over. The doll had a symbol carved into its chest and its arms were bound with red string. A poppet. She dropped the doll as if it had burned her fingers.

She heard a humming from behind the kitchen door and she pushed it open.

The Perfumier stood over the stove, stirring a pot of dark, viscous liquid, the consistency of jam.

The smell of it turned Diane's stomach. It smelled ... wrong somehow. Like mildew under wet leaves. Like death.

The Scapegoat

The city was dead, and it looked like it had been for some time. Grey dust, the last ashes of whatever civilisation used to stand there, blew in tight bundles across the pock-marked earth. The only sound was the high, keening wail of the wind as it prowled between the half-crumbled spires and minarets of the temple.

Two figures stood amongst the ruins: a young woman making notes in a book, and a young man taking photographs.

The young man looked intently through the lens of his camera, and then he spoke quietly to his companion. "Esme. There's someone else here."

The woman looked up. "Where?"

He pointed. "There's a man up by the temple. I can see him through my camera." He hesitated. "Should we speak to him?"

"Do you think it's safe?"

He took another look. "He's old and there are two of us. We should move slowly; he's probably going to be more afraid of us than we are of him."

They stowed their equipment in their bags, leaving their hands empty, and they moved in the open to give the man plenty of time to witness their approach.

By the time they reached the temple he was standing, palms flat by his sides as if he had been waiting for them for a long time.

"Who are you? Why are you here?" he asked. His voice held no anger, only curiosity.

"I'm Esme and this is Aiden. We're historians," Esme said. "We're here to find out about this place."

"You're here to find out what happened. To bear witness."

"Yes," said Aiden. "To bear witness. Exactly. I like that."

The man sighed. "It's a shameful tale," he said.

"You know what happened?" Aiden sounded incredulous. "We've never found anyone who knows what happened."

"I know."

Aiden reached into his bag and took out his camera. "Do you mind if I take some pictures?" he asked.

The old man looked askance at the camera, but then he shrugged.

Aiden took his response as permission and began to fiddle with the settings on his camera.

"Will you tell us what you know?" Esme asked.

The man sighed again. "I do not know where to begin."

Esme put a hand on his arm. "Start with your name," she suggested.

"Cyrus," the man said after a moment. "My name is Cyrus."

He had been nineteen years old the first time he went to war. Little more than a boy. He knew nothing of what it meant to go away and fight – and nothing of what it meant to come home again.

The army trudged up the hill, and he could see the city sprawled out in front of them. Part of him wanted to leave his fellow soldiers behind, to race through the gates and down to his home as fast as he could run – the way he had when he was a child. He held himself in check, forced himself to stay in formation with the others.

"We make camp here for the night."

His commanding officer's voice rang out, and all around him, men began to echo the order.

"Make camp, boys." "Break here for camp."

He felt his own mouth drop open. "Here?" The words escaped before he could stop them. "But we're only a few miles from the city. Why -"

A glare from the man nearest to him was enough to stop him from speaking further.

"Don't you know anything, boy?" The man demanded. "When you're given an order, you obey it. Now stop whining and start helping."

Cyrus eased his pack off his aching shoulders and fell into the familiar rhythms of fetching and carrying canvas tents, and of helping to drive stakes into the hard, dry earth.

It seemed to take a long time for night to fall and he noticed that none of the soldiers had taken the opportunity to look over the city while it was still light. Many of them sat with their backs to it, as if they were trying to forget that it was there at all.

"Won't the people in the city see the torches up here?" he said, almost to himself. "Won't they come looking to see whether it's us?"

The man who had shouted at him earlier gave him a long, hard stare. "They know better than to come here," he said. "Put it out of your mind."

Cyrus tried. But as the camp fell into silence around him, he found himself plagued with images of home. He remembered his mother's face on the last day he had seen her – the day he had gone away. He remembered how her lips had trembled as she told him to be careful, the expression on her face as she pressed his father's knife into his hands. She would be able to see the torches on the hill from her house. She would know what it meant. He thought that it must be a kind of torture for her - to know the army was back safely, but not to know whether her son was among them.

He sat up. Moving softly, he exited the tent and crept through the camp. There were still some men awake, talking quietly or playing cards by the light of the fires. They ignored him as he wound his way around the small groups.

He came to the edge of the camp. Shivering in the sudden cool of the night air, he crept towards the city gate.

I could be home and back again before first light, he told himself.

He was almost blind this far from the fires, and it wasn't until he was close enough to reach out and put a hand on the heavy, iron gates that he realised he wouldn't be going anywhere tonight. They were barred shut.

"You." The voice sounded from nearby, and he jumped. "What are you doing?"

"I ..." He blinked into the darkness, trying and failing to make out the man standing there. "I was ..."

The figure stepped forward and took him by the shoulder, one heavy hand clamping down firmly. "Come with me," he said.

"In here." The man pushed him forwards, into the tent.

The boy blinked and found himself face to face with a large man with a hawkish nose and thin, drawn features. He swallowed. He had never seen the man up close before, but he would have recognised General Lox anywhere.

"I'm sorry to disturb you at this hour, General," said the man who had brough him to the tent. "But I caught him trying to enter the city."

The General's eyes swivelled to meet Cyrus'. "Is that true?" he asked.

Cyrus though about lying, but one look at the General's expression made him reconsider. "Yes, Sir," he said instead.

"Who were you trying to see?"

"My mother, Sir." Cyrus felt the heat rising in his cheeks. "I thought she might be worried about me."

He half expected them to laugh at him – a boy sneaking home to see his mother – but when the General spoke, there was no trace of humour in his voice.

"By the gods, boy. You would run off to see your mother with the stain of your enemies' blood all over you? Didn't your father teach you any better?"

Cyrus spoke through gritted teeth. "My father is dead. Sir," he added hurriedly.

The General paused. "He died when you were young?"

"Yes, Sir."

"And this is your first campaign?"

"Yes, Sir."

The General exchanged a glance with the other man. "Ah," he said, after a moment. "That does go some way towards explaining your behaviour then." He sighed. "Young man, it has been a long day and I have no time for those who cannot follow orders. Berens here will take you back to your tent, where you will stay. Do not let me see you here again." He leaned over the boy. "It is not my custom to give out warnings, so consider yourself lucky you found me in a generous mood. If I have any further trouble with you, I will have you publicly whipped."

"Yes, Sir," Cyrus said. "Thank you."

The General raised a hand dismissively. He was, the boy noticed, already turning away to stare at a small leather bag perched on the corner of his desk.

Berens shoved him back into his tent.

"Stay in there," he said. "If you need to take a piss, you do it in the corner, understand? I don't want to see hide nor hair of you again tonight."

The boy rubbed at his sore shoulder and said nothing. He picked his way between the bodies of sleeping men and made his way back to his pallet. He was sure that he wouldn't be able to get to sleep, but it seemed that he had hardly closed his eyes before he heard the horns sounding, calling him to morning duties.

He followed the others out of the tent and was surprised to see them all joining one big line.

The sun was barely over the horizon and every man looked grim and tired.

General Lox was walking among the troops. He held a small, leather bag in his hand and, at every tenth man, he opened the bag and held it out.

The boy watched as each soldier reached into the bag and took something out of it. The men all opened their hands and spoke briefly to the General, who nodded and moved on.

"What's happening?" Cyrus asked.

None of the men around him said anything. None of them met his eyes.

Cyrus watched Lox making his way down the line, and he began to count the number of men between the General and himself. A cold feeling settled over him, and he counted again – praying that he was wrong, for reasons that he didn't yet understand.

And still, no one would look at him.

When the General stopped in front of Cyrus, he gave no indication that he recognised the boy from the previous night. He held open the bag and motioned to it without speaking.

Cyrus put his hand into the bag, and felt cool, hard objects nestled inside. He closed his fingers around one of them, drawing it out.

"Show me," the General said. His voice was firm, but not unkind.

Cyrus opened his hand. Balanced on his palm was an ordinary grey pebble.

The General nodded, just as he had done with all the others, and moved on.

The soldiers standing on either side of the boy seemed to exhale as one. The younger one, standing to his right, turned to him as if he was about to speak.

They were interrupted by a low wail.

Cyrus turned to see the soldier standing ten men down from him with his palm upturned and his face rigid. The pebble on his palm was a dark, rusty red – the colour of an open wound.

The General reached out and closed the man's fingers over the pebble, hiding it from view. He leaned forward and said something, his voice low and gentle, his words too quiet for Cyrus to hear.

The man's shoulders sagged, and he nodded.

The men on either side of him stepped forward and led him away.

"You were here when all this happened?" Aiden asked. "How is that possible?"

"What did the red stone mean?" Esme asked, her voice tense.

The old man stared at the horizon, as if he was seeing a different sky.

"Red for blood," he said, almost to himself. "Red for death."

The soldiers filed one by one to a tent in the centre of the camp, near to where Cyrus had been brought the night before. The tent was small and had a symbol daubed on the front in red ink.

Berens strode over and slipped into the line ahead of Cyrus. Nobody complained.

"Do you know what to do?" he asked.

Cyrus shook his head.

"You have been to confession before? At the temple?"

"Yes."

"When you go in there you must confess every sin you have committed during the course of this gods-blasted war." He spat on the ground and then glared at the boy. "Every one, mind you. Leave nothing out, no matter how small. You don't want to carry any of this back to your family."

Cyrus wanted to ask more questions, but Berens was already being ushered inside the tent.

He was inside for a long time, and he did not look at the boy as he came out.

When it was his turn, Cyrus moved quickly, ducking his head as he entered the tent. He wrinkled his nose as the cloying scent of burning herbs threatened to choke him. He could barely see the man through the grey smoke, but he knew it was the same one who had taken the red pebble.

There was a moment's silence, and then the boy began to speak. He was hesitant at first, but then he spoke faster and faster, becoming almost eager to vomit up his sins, his cruelty, his cowardice.

The man remained silent until after he had finished speaking, and then he said, "I have heard your sins and I will bear the burden of them on your behalf." His voice was flat and raspy.

"Thank you," said the boy – because he didn't know what else to say.

He ducked back outside and heaved in a lungful of fresh air.

It was almost mid-day when they brought the man with the red pebble to the edge of the camp. Someone had worked to build a wooden platform, and it stood in the shade of a nearby tree. As if, thought Cyrus, someone had placed it there to provide some comfort from the unforgiving sun blazing overhead.

The boy watched as the man was led onto the platform. His eyes were wide in his pale face and his hands were visibly shaking, but his pace was steady as he climbed.

The other men clustered around them. They weren't like soldiers standing in formation, they were more like the crowds at a market, jostling for the best views.

The man knelt on the platform and the General climbed up beside him.

Again, he spoke in that low, comforting tone, and again the man seemed to calm.

Again the boy was unable to make out any of the words.

He saw the knife flash and, in the instant before the General struck, Cyrus realised what was about to happen. He felt himself raise a hand - as if to ward it off - but it was too late.

General Lox drew the knife across the man's throat in one smooth motion.

The man grabbed at his throat, as if was trying to stem the blood that poured from it. It seeped out from between his fingers, falling from the platform and staining the stones below it a dark, rusty red.

"They were all the same," the old man said quietly. "They all cried and wept at first and then later they seemed to calm down and accept their fates."

"How many?" asked Esme. She had long since removed her hand from Cyrus' arm.

"Six in my lifetime."

"Six!"

"You don't understand. You think their deaths were meaningless, but you're wrong. They took our sins with them to the grave. They kept our families safe."

"Safe from what?" Aiden asked.

The old man turned his cloudy eyes in Aiden's direction. "Safe from us," he said. "That's why the gates were barred, why we were forbidden from entering the city until after the ritual." He paused. "Have you ever been to war?"

"No," Aiden said.

Esme shook her head.

"You do things in war. Things that make you ashamed. Things that leave a stain on your soul. You should never carry any of that back to your family. The sins of the evildoer must never be laid at the feet of the innocent, you understand?" His voice had taken on an urgent quality.

"So, these men took on your sins?" Aiden asked. "They were your sacrifices."

"Your scapegoats," Esme said quietly.

"Yes."

Aiden gestured at the dead city. "What happened?" he asked.

Cyrus closed his eyes. "We chose the wrong man," he said.

There was something wrong with the man in the tent – the man who had chosen the red pebble. Instead of waiting quietly among the burning herbs, he laughed and gibbered to himself – and occasionally broke out into a bawdy drinking song.

"Lost his mind," the soldiers whispered. "The fear has sent him mad."

"A bad portent," muttered others, "to have a madman carry our sins."

The whole camp turned out to watch his execution, but the crowd was quieter than usual, and they stood further away from the platform. Several of the men chose to stand on the far side of the platform, pressed closely in among the trees. No one stopped them. No one insisted they take their usual places in the sun-lit clearing.

"It was," Cyrus told Aiden and Esme, "as if we were trying to hide our shame from the gods themselves."

The man with the red pebble scaled the platform, unaided. A wide grin was stretched across his features, lending shadows to his face and giving it an odd sense of proportion. He swept his manic gaze across the crowd.

No one would meet his eyes.

When he saw the General approaching, the man let out a high-pitched giggle and, instead of kneeling, he leaned back slightly, pulling his longish hair away from his neck – as if he was offering his throat for cutting. He started laughing again – and he was still laughing as the General drew the knife across his throat.

He continued to laugh until the laughter turned to gurgling sounds and his blood stained the stones below.

It was three days before anything happened. Three days in which the returning soldiers visited the temple, drank with their friends, and spent time in the gardens with their loved ones.

Cyrus was woken around midnight by the sound of running in the street outside his house. He looked out of his window and saw the source of the trouble straight away; the torches were all burning outside the temple, giving the gold-plated dome an eerie glow that made it look almost as if it was burning.

He dressed quickly and made his way outside, following the sounds of shouting that drifted towards him on the breeze.

Outside the temple, a priest was sitting on the ground. His robes were torn and covered in dirt, and his face was buried in his hands.

One of the guards was trying to speak to him, but the priest refused to look up.

Cyrus passed them and continued to follow the sounds of the shouting.

Inside the temple, all was chaos. Urns and vases had been upturned; their contents spilled onto the floor. Precious shrines and relics had been smashed. There was a trail of blood smeared darkly across one wall, and when Cyrus looked more closely, he realised that there was an obscene word written in the blood. He shuddered and backed away.

He made his way into one of the temple's antechambers.

A body lay on the ground. It was partially covered by a soldier's cloak, but the sandal-shod feet visible at the bottom suggested to Cyrus that the body was that of one of the priests.

On the far side of the chamber, two guards held a man pinned up against the wall. The man's hands were covered in blood and streaks of it covered one side of his head – as if he had run his bloody hands through his close-cropped hair. He hung loosely in the guards' grip and seemed to be making no attempt to flee.

The man looked up and saw Cyrus.

"I had to!" he shouted. "You were there. You saw. My sin," he croaked, his voice breaking. "My sins. All my sins." He lapsed into muttering.

Cyrus felt his stomach twist, felt bile rise in his throat. He watched in silence as the guards dragged the man away.

Three nights later, he was walking in the city, unable to sleep, when he rounded a corner and saw fire in the distance. People were already running in the direction of the smoke and Cyrus followed the crowd to find that two houses were alight. The city guards had already begun to organised bucket-chains and Cyrus joined the line, passing water to the men at the front.

He could see that it was already too late to save one of the houses – the roof had collapsed inwards, sending showers of red-hot ash into the night sky.

A man was outside, being held back from entering the house by a small group.

"He did it," a woman cried, pointing at the man as he tried to push his way into the ruined building. "He set the fire. I saw him."

"My wife," the man screamed. "My children. My sins, my sins. All of my sins." He let out a high-pitched laugh and slumped into the arms of the crowd.

Cyrus watched as the angry mob descended.

"Their sins?" Aiden frowned.

"The first man desecrated a temple in an enemy city. The second burned a family in their beds. These were the sins they confessed before they returned home. These were the sins that came back to haunt them."

"And the rest?" Aiden asked.

"All of us. We were all compelled to act out our sins."

"Why didn't you leave?"

"We tried. We couldn't make ourselves walk through the gates. Then we tried to send away the women and children, but they couldn't leave either. It was as if some force was holding them here. With us."

"Stop it," Esme said. She sounded as though she might be sick. "I don't want to hear any more."

The old man nodded. He was silent for a moment and then he said, "It's growing dark, and the city is difficult to navigate at night. I can take you as far as the gates."

Esme turned to Aiden. "What if we can't leave?"

"We had nothing to do with any of this."

"Neither did his children."

In response, Aiden set off walking.

Esme and Cyrus followed, with Esme keeping as much distance as possible between herself and the old man.

"I have to know," Aiden said. "What was your sin."

Cyrus stopped. "Nothing," he said.

"Nothing? I don't -"

"I knew what they were doing - those other soldiers. I knew that first man desecrated a temple. I knew the other man murdered a family. I knew because I saw them do it - and I did nothing to stop them. My sin was the sin of inaction."

"That's why you're still here," Esme said. "You were forced to watch and do nothing while everyone else died." She put a shaking hand on the old man's shoulder. "That's horrible."

Ahead of them, Aiden started to laugh.

Esme frowned. "Aiden? What are you doing?"

Aiden turned, and in the dying light a grin was visible on his face. It stretched across his features, lending shadows to his face and giving it an odd sense of proportion. He let out another laugh and then he lunged at Esme, wrapping his hands around her throat.

She tumbled backwards into the dust, with Aiden still on top of her.

"Help me," she managed to choke out, her eyes finding Cyrus' face.

"I can't," he said. "Don't you understand? It's my sin repeating itself. My sins. All of my sins."

A Rum Affair

Elizabeth Abercromby sat on the harbour wall, bare feet swinging below her, and tried to catch her breath. She should have been practising her Latin, she knew, but the thought of being stuck indoors on such a beautiful day held little enough appeal for her without adding the thought of her Governess hovering over her, ready to chide her for the smallest mistake in subjunctive clauses or verb tenses.

She laughed a little to herself as she thought of the way she had waited until the woman was distracted, engaged in conversation with one of the footmen, before she had made her way quietly to the door. The Governess had turned as she was easing her way through the partially open door, left ajar to enable a slight draft to offer some relief from the stifling heat of the classroom. She had lunged for Elizabeth, uttering a most unladylike curse as she did so, but Bess had skipped nimbly out of the older woman's reach and had taken off at full speed down the corridor and into the courtyard, her skirts pulled up scandalously high to avoid tripping on them as she ran. Bess imagined the Governess stalking through the town, red-faced, with her turkey neck wobbling the way it always did when she was angry – which was often. She would make her way to the harbour eventually, Bess knew, and at that point she would be better returning to her studies lest the Governess involve her father, but for now she had bought herself some peace and quiet sitting in the sunshine watching the fishing boats bob up and down on the clear, blue waves.

Lost in self-satisfied daydreams, Bess suddenly frowned and squinted into the sunlight. There was something about one of the ships that had caught her attention. It looked wrong somehow – the size of it and the way it moved, faster than the little fishing boats but in a way that struck her as being more haphazard. She continued to watch the boat as it headed towards the harbour, far too quickly, almost as though it didn't intend to stop when it reached the little jetty, almost as though its inhabitants intended to beach themselves somehow. Reflexively, Bess brought a hand to her mouth, smothering a gasp as she watched the boat approach.

"Got you!"

Bess almost screamed as she felt a hand clamp down on her wrist. Her Governess, just as red in the face as Bess had expected and panting with the exertion of having made her way from the big house on the hill down into the harbour in the blazing sun, was gripping her, nails digging into Bess' skin and a hideous look of triumph on her face.

"Now you just come with me, young miss," she began, twisting Bess' wrist a little to let her know she was serious. "Or your father will hear all about..." Abruptly she stopped speaking, her jaw dropping as she stared at the jetty beyond them.

Bess turned, following the Governess' gaze and her heart missed a beat. Somehow, the boat had managed to weigh anchor just before it crashed into the little jetty and a line of men were streaming out of it. That might have been concerning enough on its own, but there was no missing the main activity on the deck. As Bess watched, several men hauled on ropes and a flag began to rise on the flagpole. A black flag, with an unmistakeable threat embroidered into it. Beside her the

Governess gasped loudly and let go of Bess' wrist, using her free hand to make the sign of the cross above herself.

"Lord have mercy," she whispered.

Bess leapt from the wall, landing next to the frightened woman, and gave her a little push.

"Run," she said.

The woman merely stared at her, mouth agape. Bess pushed her again, harder this time.

"Grey. We have to go back to the house. Now."

She'd used her last name, the way her father did when he wanted to make a point. This time the woman nodded, her eyes still on the rapidly approaching group of men. Without stopping to pick up her shoes, Bess grabbed her Governess by the wrist and started to run, half dragging the woman behind her.

They didn't even make it out of the harbour. They rounded a corner, Bess still trying to chivvy her Governess along and almost ran smack into a small group of men.

"Well now..." A skinny man in mismatched, patchwork clothing grinned at them, exposing a crooked, gummy smile. "What do we have here?"

Grey let out a small squeak, which Bess ignored.

"We have no quarrel with you... gentlemen," she said. "I'm just on my way to take this woman home. As you can plainly see from her face, she is unwell."

The man's eyes flicked from Bess to Grey and his smile widened. Bess took a deep breath and made as if to move past him, whereupon the smile vanished instantly from his face and he grabbed her by both shoulders, blocking her path completely.

"Did I say you could go anywhere?" he demanded.

Bess felt herself reddening. "I wasn't aware that I needed your permission to visit my own home, sir," she said.

The man laughed, shaking her for good measure. Behind him, his cronies were leaning forwards, predatory grins on all their faces.

"Do you have any idea to whom you are speaking?" Grey's voice rang out from behind Bess, quavering with indignation. "That is the Lady Elizabeth Abercromby, and you will take your hands off her immediately, you vile little man!"

Inwardly, Bess groaned. Grey had picked a fine time to rediscover her voice, she thought.

"Is it now?" The man's eyes narrowed as he appraised Bess' dress, her jewellery. "And what would you say she's worth, this Lady Elizabeth Abercromby of yours?"

"I ... I," Grey stuttered.

"For God's sake, Grey, be quiet," Bess hissed. "Sir," she said turning back to the man. "I'm sure that there is some arrangement that we can come to here. There is no need for any violence." Her voice caught a little over the last word.

"Got a rich husband, do you?" he sneered.

Bess shook her head.

The man ran his tongue over what remained of his bottom teeth and nodded.

"Better hope you have a rich daddy then, your ladyship."

"She does," Grey squeaked. "Oh indeed, her father is very rich, very well-respected in these parts. I'm sure he will be more than happy to..."

"Somebody shut her up," the man said. "Her voice is getting on my nerves."

One of the other men stepped around Bess and swung his fist at Grey, catching her in the temple and sending her sprawling to the ground.

Bess glared at the man, her eyes flashing defiance.

"That, sir, was incredibly stupid," she said.

"Eh?"

Bess didn't know whether he was shocked by her less than conciliatory tone or whether he genuinely didn't understand what he had just done, but she ploughed on regardless.

"It is clearly your intention to kidnap me and claim a ransom from my father, am I correct?" she asked. "You were asking about my worth and since I doubt you are here to offer me your hand in marriage, it follows that you are planning to hold me for ransom, yes?"

The man nodded, dumbly. Behind him, one of the other men sniggered.

"Well then. Just who do you suppose is going to take that message to my father, since you have just rendered unconscious the only person besides myself who knows where he is and would be able to deliver such a message without immediately being arrested?"

"The girl has a point," one of the men said, the one who had been laughing behind his back.

The man swore and glared at Bess, all trace of humour gone from his face. Several seconds ticked by while he weighed up his options. Bess could practically see the cogs moving in his mind.

"Get her to the ship," he said eventually, with a low growl.

Before Bess could protest any further the big man, the one who had felled Grey, lifted her and slung her over one shoulder with no more care or effort than if she had been a bag of flour.

Bess ground her teeth against the indignity of it and could only be glad that most of the town currently had more pressing things to do than gawp at the Lady Elizabeth Abercromby being hauled around like a peasant's wife.

She woke in a cramped and somewhat smelly cabin sometime after the sun had set. She stretched out in an experimental fashion and was relieved to find that all her limbs seemed to be intact – something that had felt less than assured as she was being bounced through the town a few hours earlier. She also found that wherever they had taken her was small enough that she could reach both sides of it without having to try too hard. Gingerly, she sat up and immediately hit her head on something above her.

"Blood and thunder!" she cursed, holding a hand to her injured forehead. Thankfully, it came away without any of the tell-tale stickiness that would have suggested she was bleeding.

A door swung open to her left, allowing a small amount of light into the cabin. It was enough for Bess to see that she had been left in the lower bunk of a set of beds attached to the wall. She had hit her head on the upper bunk when she tried to rise, she realised.

"Miss? Are you alright down there?"

"Quite alright, thank you," she muttered.

A head appeared around the door, and she recognised the younger of the men from the harbour.

"Are you sure? I heard you swearing." He hesitated and then shot her a conspiratorial, almost friendly grin. "Never knew ladies swore like that."

Bess smiled back.

"You would be surprised what ladies get up to," she said.

It might have been her imagination, but she thought she detected a faint blush on his cheeks.

"Are you hungry?" he asked, after a moment. "The grub's not fancy but I can get you something if you want it?"

Bess made up her mind in a rush.

"Do I have to stay here? In this cabin, I mean. I'd much rather go up on deck."

The boy looked dubious. "I'm not sure that's a good idea, miss."

"Please. What's your name?"

"Jim."

"Please, Jim. I'm in dire need of fresh air. And besides, I've never been out to sea before. I'd dearly love to take a look at the scenery."

He laughed.

"Not much scenery this time of night, miss. Even the stars are staying hidden this time of year."

"Please," she said again.

He smiled.

"Alright, miss. I can't see no harm in it as long as you stay with me."

She beamed at him, stood carefully and offered him her arm as though he was going to be escorting her to the Autumn Ball instead of the deck of a pirate ship. He flashed her another grin, made a half bow, and took her by the arm, leading her out into the cool night air.

There were lights on deck, she saw, oil lamps burning dimly by the rigging. In the dark night it might have been enough to give away their position, but she guessed they were far enough out to sea that it would take quite some time for anyone to approach them. She assumed that they would have posted a watch to make sure that no one could get close to them without being spotted, and she had seen for herself how swiftly the ship could move if it needed to. There were several men on deck, hauling at ropes, moving boxes or just lying around, arms behind their heads as makeshift pillows. Many of them glanced curiously at her as she walked past. One or two of them whistled, quiet and low and half-heartedly menacing. Beside her, Jim was explaining the layout of the deck, pausing only if they had to step around a sleeping pirate.

"This here is the main rigging. And over there, on that rise, is the ship's wheel. The mess is down thataway."

She nodded along with him, focusing on walking on the deck which seemed to shift below her feet, sometimes rising so sharply she felt she might be thrown into the air at any moment and other times falling, giving her the impression that there was empty air between herself and the wooden boards. Once or twice she tightened her grip on Jim and he pressed her arm as if to reassure her.

"Takes time to get your sea legs, miss," he said. "You should have seen me my first week aboard ship. Pretty sure I spent the whole time green around the gills."

"Any tips for how to get my 'sea legs' faster?" she asked.

"Well, usually I'd tell you to focus on the horizon but ..." He gestured to the inky darkness over the side of the ship.

"Oh," she half laughed. "Perhaps I should have taken your advice and come up here in the daytime."

He seemed on the verge of saying something else, when he saw something over her shoulder and he straightened slightly, pulling his face into a serious expression.

"What the hell is she doing up here?"

The skinny man from the harbour, with the bad teeth, strode towards them. A long coat, at least two sizes too big for him was hanging from his thin frame and a black tricorn hat was balanced on his head. The overall effect was much like watching a child who had dressed as a pirate, and Bess struggled to smother a smile as he approached.

"She wanted to see the deck, Captain," said Jim.

Captain? Bess thought. *This inept little man?*

"I don't care what she wanted, boy! This isn't a pleasure cruise. She's a damned prisoner!" Spittle flew from the captain's mouth as he shouted.

"It's really my fault, Captain," Bess interjected smoothly. "I struggle terribly in cramped places, you see. They make me quite ill."

The captain leered at her.

"Your comfort ain't my first concern here, your ladyship," he said.

"But my health should be," she replied.

That brought him up short.

"Your health," he repeated.

"Of course. I'm your Golden Goose, so to speak."

He blinked at her.

"Money, Captain," she said in a tone of voice that one might use on a small child. "You want my father to pay money for my safe return. No safe return, no money."

All around them, men were sitting up on the deck, watching her with eyes that had brightened at her words.

"Alright then. You can come up on deck to 'take the air' or whatever it is you rich girls do." He smiled as he indicated the men around them. "I'd stick close to young Jim here though. The rest of my crew might not be as... polite as he is."

His meaning was clear, and Bess' lips thinned as she considered his words. Finally, she nodded.

"Good then." He smiled again and raised his voice for the benefit of his crew. "We're going to make some money off you, your ladyship. Twenty talents at least."

"Fifty," she said, coolly.

"Eh?"

"Fifty talents, Captain. That's how much you should ask for."

The captain's jaw dropped, and Bess could hear muttering among the watching men.

"It's been a long day, Captain, and I'm quite tired. Jim, could you escort me back to my cabin please?"

Jim glanced at his captain but when it became obvious that he was too lost in thought to either approve or deny Bess' request, he merely shrugged and led the way back across the deck.

"Goodnight, Captain," Bess called over her shoulder.

From somewhere behind her, she heard something that sounded suspiciously like laughter.

"What made you choose this life, Jim?" Bess asked. It had been three days since she had been brought aboard the ship and she was standing against the railings, watching the horizon. Jim had been right, it had helped a little, and the swaying of the deck no longer made her feel like she might embarrass herself in front of the men.

"Piracy, you mean?" Jim asked.

"I might not have phrased it quite so indelicately."

He laughed. "That's alright, I know what I am."

"But why choose it though?"

He sighed. "I took the silver," he said.

"I don't understand."

"I was drinking in a bar one night and when I got to the bottom of the cup, there was a silver coin in it."

"Why would anyone put a silver coin in your cup?"

"It's how they get you, miss. Drop a coin in your drink and then tell you that you've taken the King's silver and you're in the navy now."

Bess pressed a hand to her mouth. "That's terrible."

Jim nodded. "That's not the word I used, miss, but it'll do," he said.

"So, you ran away?"

"Aye. I thought since I was going to sea either way, it might as well be on my terms." Anger flashed in his eyes for a moment making him look suddenly much older. Then he laughed, covering his anger with a smile. "Thought I'd seek my fame and fortune and then retire somewhere hot where I could enjoy it."

Bess eyed his patchwork trousers. "It seems you're still seeking it," she said.

He shrugged. "We were doing alright under the old captain. And then Hobbes, he's the new captain, took over and..."

"He hasn't found his sea legs yet?" Bess suggested gently.

Jim snorted. "Right enough, miss," he said.

"Bess," she corrected. "My friends call me Bess."

Jim beamed at her. "Well then, Bess. We best get you down to the mess or all the good slop'll be gone."

They were still in the mess when the door was flung open and Captain Hobbes slammed into the room, a thunderous expression on his face and a piece of parchment in his hand.

"Proof of life!" he practically screamed in Bess' face, his breath stinking of booze. "Your father wants something called 'proof of life' before he'll send us one single talent!"

Bess rolled her eyes. "That's dear old daddy for you. He wants to be certain of his investment before he parts with his money."

"Think this is funny? You promised us fifty talents, girl." His eyes narrowed. "You said you were worth it. Staked your health on it, as I remember."

Bess ignored the thumping that had started in her chest. "Calm down, Captain. We simply do as he says."

"How? You'll not be setting foot on the mainland until I see my money. I won't be fooled by the likes of you!" he spat. "Or maybe you suggest I commission an artist to draw a portrait of you reclining on the deck of my ship." He held a hand up the way one might hold a cup of tea, little finger raised in the air.

That's it.

"A finger," Bess said sounding calmer than she felt.

"A what?"

"You cut off my finger, Captain, and send it to him. Preferably with one of the pieces of jewellery that you took from me when you brought me on board. That's how he will know I'm alive."

"You want me to cut off your finger?" he repeated.

"Bess, are you sure?" Jim asked.

Bess ignored Jim, focusing all her attention on Hobbes. "Unless you don't feel that you're up to it. In which case, hand me a cutlass and I'll do it myself."

Hobbes crouched down, drawing his face level with hers so that he could look directly into her eyes.

"I've done worse things than cut off a finger, your ladyship."

All around them, the room had gone silent. The only noise to be heard was the ever-present lapping of the sea at the hull.

"I don't doubt it," Bess said. "So, there should be no problem." She laid her left hand, palm down on the table in front of her. "Quickly please," she said, tightly.

Hobbes stared at her for a moment and then uncoupled the cutlass from his belt. He squinted down at her hand.

"Captain," Jim began, nervously, but Bess shushed him.

"Hush, Jim. Captain Hobbes needs to concentrate. If he takes off my whole hand I'll bleed to death, and he won't get his coin."

Hobbes raised his eyes back to her face, his own face draining of colour. His hands were visibly shaking. The whole room seemed to hold its breath as he wavered.

"Oh really, Captain Hobbes, must you make such a fuss about this? It's not as though you are the one losing a finger. Here," Bess continued, "let me do it."

She held out a hand and Hobbes, as if in a trance, slowly handed her the sword. One of the men, the big one from the harbour, half rose from his seat. Before anyone had time to act, Bess closed four of her fingers into a fist, leaving only her little finger exposed and brought the cutlass down on the table. There was a sickening crunch and the top part of her finger rolled away, cleanly severed at the knuckle, leaving a trail of blood behind it on the table.

"Blood and thunder!" Bess dropped the sword and cradled her mutilated left hand, closing her eyes.

"Jesus, Bess!" Jim grabbed a rag and prised her hand open, wrapping it round her finger to try to staunch the bleeding.

The big man picked up the fallen cutlass and handed it back to Hobbes without ever taking his eyes off Bess.

Hobbes took the sword without a word. Then he picked up Bess' finger from the table and looked around the room, as if waiting to be told what to do with it. After a moment, he half nodded at Bess and swept out of the room.

"Are you alright?" Jim asked.

Bess patted him lightly on the hand, unwound the makeshift bandage and then turned to the big man. "Is that rum in your cup?"

He nodded.

She held out her right hand. "May I?" she asked.

He passed her the cup, and she poured a little over her finger, swearing again as the alcohol hit the wound. As they watched, she took a huge swig, coughing slightly as the liquid hit the back of her throat.

"Thank you," she said, handing the cup back. There was something new in his eyes as he looked at her, she thought. Something that looked an awful lot like respect.

Before too long, she was doing an awfully good impression of a woman who had drunk far too much rum. In reality, she had only taken small sips before she passed the cup to the man next to her, but she copied their slurred speech, their jaunty way of raising the cup as if toasting each sip they took from it, and she laughed uproariously at their dirty jokes.

"So, tell me," she slurred, passing the cup to a man with a shock of dark hair and a face like a rat. "What in the world did you do to deserve a captain like Hobbes?"

Several of the men glanced furtively at one another and for a moment Bess thought she might have overstepped.

"He killed the old captain," the big man said, the first time Bess had heard him speak.

"On purpose?" she asked dryly, and the man smiled.

"That's how it works here, Bessie," Jim said, eyes rolling in his head as he talked. "You don't like the captain, you take matters into your own hands. And then you're the captain."

"In that case, I find it difficult to believe no one has done for him yet," she said, attempting to imitate their idioms. "If the man can't even take a finger from a woman who isn't resisting, how is he going to lead you to glory?"

"To glory!" one of the men shouted, raising the cup in the air.

The others repeated the chant, laughing, but Bess could see that even in their rum induced haze, some of the men were considering what she had said.

She rose from the table, careful to seem a little unsteady on her feet and made her excuses. Jim was in no fit state to walk her back to the cabin, but on balance Bess decided she was probably safe to go alone. As she made her way across the deck, she fancied she could almost see the harbour lights like tiny fireflies in the distance.

Bess heard Jim groaning before she saw him. The sun was high in the sky, and she was leaning over the railings, breathing in the fresh sea air and enjoying the slight burning sensation of the salt on her tongue. It was almost enough to distract from the throbbing pain in her finger, if she concentrated hard enough.

Jim looked like he might have recently spent time leaning over the railing for an entirely different reason.

"How are you standing there like that?" he demanded, leaning on the railing next to her. "You're fresh as a daisy."

Bess shrugged. "I felt a little poorly earlier, but it was nothing that some fresh air couldn't fix."

"Never known anything like it," Jim said, glancing at her sideways.

"The pirate life must agree with me."

"Looks like. But you'll be going home once your father gets…" he trailed off, his face turning even greener. "His proof you're alive," he finished lamely.

Home, she thought. *Back to ballgowns and conjugating Latin verbs, and a father who made me cut off my own finger just to live another day.*

Bess turned away to stare out over the endless, sparkling sea.

It was late when the captain breezed into her cabin. Bess had been lying on her bunk, allowing the soft

82

rocking motion of the waves to send her sleep when the door opened, and Hobbes appeared.

"Your lucky day, girl," he grinned.

"Captain Hobbes. Won't you come in?"

His grin faltered. "Think you're clever, don't you, girl."

She sat up, aware of how alone she was, how confined the space was.

"I take it you've agreed terms." She kept her tone carefully neutral.

He stared at her for a long moment, long enough that she began to think she had pressed her luck with him one too many times, but then he nodded as if to accept her change of subject. "Your father will send a man with the money. Then we drop you off on Rook's Island. Someone will come and get you." He shrugged and his grin widened again. "Probably."

"When?" she asked.

"Tomorrow. Soon as we get our gold." He made as if to leave and then looked back at her. "You've been a thorn in my side, your ladyship, and I'll be glad to get rid of you. Dangerous waters round Rook's Island too. Be a right shame if you were to drown before you made it to dry land."

He closed the door, leaving her in darkness. Bess waited for several long minutes to make sure he had really gone, then she eased herself out of her bunk and crept outside. She leaned over the railings and listened to the waves rise and fall in the pitch black. She wished she could see the stars, but Jim had been right, the skies were

83

clouded this time of year. She wished she could see home but she was too far away.

He means to kill me, she thought. *No matter what I do, I'm going to die at sea.*

She set her shoulders and turned away from the railing, walking in the direction of Jim's bunk.

Well then. Might as well be on my terms.

Bess watched as her father's man rowed away from the ship. They must be closer to home than she thought, she realised. Or at least close to Rook's Island. She had vaguely recognised the man as he nodded to her, apparently content that she was relatively unharmed. He had deposited the money with a smirking Captain Hobbes and then turned and almost run back to his boat, without ever making eye contact with her, let alone trying to speak to her. She felt strangely calm, almost peaceful, as she watched him leave; the last vestiges of her life sailing away from her.

Hobbes was elated, almost cackling as he ran the gold coins through his fingers.

"We're rich, lads," he called. "Rich beyond our wildest dreams." He turned and locked eyes with Bess, his meaning clear in his burgeoning smile. He opened his mouth, and she knew the order that would be coming, steeled herself against it.

"Shame you'll not live to spend any of it, Hobbes," Jim's voice rang out.

"Eh?" Hobbes dropped the coins, and his hand flew to his cutlass. "You can't seriously be meaning to challenge me, boy." He laughed. "See what I just did for this crew?"

"Except you didn't do any of it," Bess said.

Hobbes rounded on her. "You shut your mouth!"

"Bess is right," Jim said. "You tried to get us less than what we were owed for her, she had to tell you herself what she was worth. She cut off her own finger when your hands were shaking like a maid at her first tumble. Seems to me you didn't have much to do with any of that."

Hobbes roared and drew his cutlass – only to find that every man on the deck did the same. He blinked. "Mutiny? You ungrateful sons of whores!"

"You have a choice, Hobbes. You can take the honourable way out, or we can cut you down where you stand." Jim's voice was calm.

Hobbes blanched.

"The plank?" he asked.

"Aye. The plank."

Hobbes straightened. "I'll not let you bastards run me through. I'd rather take my chances in the water."

The big man and two others stepped forward, disarmed Hobbes and started to lead him away.

"Wait a moment, please," Bess called.

Hobbes turned with hope in his eyes.

Bess crossed the short space between them and stood on her tiptoes so she could whisper in Hobbes' ear, "Be careful, Mister Hobbes, dangerous waters round here." Then she smiled and plucked the tricorn hat from his head. "I rather like this," she announced. "It's quite jaunty. I think I'll wear it myself."

Bess didn't look back as they led him away.

Sometime after they heard the sound of Hobbes going into the water – a long drawn-out expletive that was cut off by a loud splash – Jim asked Bess what she was going to do now.

"I thought I might seek my fame and fortune with you here," she told him. "Elizabeth Abercromby is dead, but the fearsome Nine Fingered Bess is just getting started."

This story first appeared in the 'Harvey Duckman Presents' Pirate-themed special, published in September 2020.

By Firelight

It was raining outside. Not that heavy downpour, thunder-and-lightning, world ending stuff; just a light, persistent drizzle that soaked everything in the immediate vicinity. Coupled with an unseasonable cold front that had hit the area overnight it made for an unpleasant, uncomfortable experience.

The man in the cabin had lived through worse. He had seen days so hot that his unprotected skin had cracked like clay in the heat and nights so cold he'd awaken to find his boots frozen to his feet - the chill of it having made ice out of his sweat as he'd slept. He had spent days without food and months without seeing another human being and both of these things had, in their time, left him wracked and twisted in pain. He had suffered a great deal worse than a light drizzle and a chill in the air, and yet somehow tonight it was unbearable. It was as if the damp night air had seeped into his bones and leached the warmth right out of them.

In almost three years of living out here the man had never approached anyone for help and had mostly stayed away from the holiday cabins that littered the woods. It was a matter of choice – he had come up here to be away from the world, and he knew better than most that humans can be dangerous, cruel animals. But something about this night had stretched his resolve past breaking point.

At first he thought that he would just go to the cabin and if nobody was home he would sleep on the porch. It would be better insulated than the ground and he would be gone before anybody noticed. But, having dragged his tired, aching body through the woods, once he finally reached the cabin he couldn't stop himself from trying the door. And so, the man stood in the cabin. Having come this far it did not stretch his principles much further to make up a small fire on the hearth. *After all*, he reasoned, *the whole endeavour would have been pointless if I broke into someone's home only to freeze to death anyway.* He was beginning to warm up and he was starting to reason out an argument for stealing a little food when he heard a noise outside.

He froze for a moment, but nothing happened. He frowned as he strained to hear any movement outside. Just as he was about to convince himself that the interruption was all in his head, the door swung open with a loud bang. The light from the fire revealed two shapes in the doorway. The man froze. The shapes froze. Then one of the shapes moved forwards, far enough into the light to reveal that it was a young woman. She couldn't' have been more than twenty-five and she was slim and pale in the flickering light.

"Please," the man tried to say. "Please." His voice was rusted with lack of use, and it came out as an inarticulate bleat.

The woman eyed him carefully, as if he were a wild animal. She took a slow step forward, her hands raised in front of her, palms out, protecting herself.

"You're not supposed to be in here." Her tone was surprisingly gentle.

He shook his head, not trusting his voice to work.

"Ben," she called over her shoulder and the other shape moved.

"Please." The man tried again. This time it was a little better, this time it came out as a whisper.

The woman's eyes moved past him to the small fire burning in the fireplace.

"Ben," she said again. "We have a guest. See if you can find something for a hot drink while I build up the fire."

Ben paused for a moment and then moved into the kitchen without a word and began sorting through cupboards.

The woman gestured at a chair. "Sit down," she said. "I'm Emma by the way."

The man looked pointedly at the immaculate chairs and then down at his own dirty trousers.

Emma followed his gaze.

"It doesn't matter, I can always get them cleaned. Besides, if you stand up for much longer you're going to fall down."

He nodded his thanks and sank gratefully into the nearest chair.

"So, what should I call you?" Emma asked as she knelt by the fire.

The question knocked him off kilter. He had owned many names but none of them seemed to fit anymore. And his birth name, the one that should have stayed with him through everything, would mark him out as something terrible. Something these people would no longer be willing to help. He cleared his throat and gave her the most generic name he could think of.

"Smith," he said. It was a name that belonged to no one. Something that marked him out as being nothing.

"Well, Mr Smith -"

"Not 'Mr' Smith. Just Smith." His words sounded harsh to his own ears, but if she noticed then she didn't seem offended.

"Well then, Smith," she began again brightly. "How did you come to be outside on a night like this?"

He was saved from having to answer the question by Ben's reappearance. Now that he could see him more clearly, the man judged Ben to be in his late twenties, with a build that might once have suggested honest work but now seemed more likely to be the result of exercise classes and health supplements.

"There wasn't any coffee," Ben said. "Only tea. I hope that's alright?" he seemed to direct the question only to Emma.

"We probably shouldn't drink coffee this late at night anyway," she replied, smiling. "Ben, this is Smith," she continued, as smoothly as if she was introducing two acquaintances at a cocktail party. Ben nodded and handed Smith a mug of tea. He didn't say anything, but Smith noticed the slight wrinkle of his nose as he leaned in.

"Smith is going to be staying here tonight," Emma said.

He felt a jolt of surprise and he saw outright dismay on Ben's face. He opened his mouth to protest but Emma silenced him with one raised finger.

"I insist," she said in a tone of finality.

Smith took a sip of his tea, not bothering to hide the grin that stretched across his face.

Little rich girl is used to getting what she wants, son. Better get used to it.

"Right then." Ben said. "I'll go and find somewhere for him to sleep."

Smith took note of the barely concealed anger on Ben's face as he left.

Emma remained kneeling by the fire as he cradled the hot mug of tea in his hands. She was angled slightly away from him, and he found himself staring at the graceful arc of her neck, marvelling at anyone who would willingly turn their back on a stranger. He had a feeling though that she was not as unaware of his attention as she was pretending to be. There was a slight shakiness to her movements – as if she was forcing herself to move slowly to demonstrate her trust in him. Even from this angle he could see that her jaw was clenched tightly closed and he wondered whether she was afraid that her teeth would chatter. With Ben out of the room she was all alone with him, and Smith allowed the fact of her closeness to intrude on his awareness.

91

Both Smith and Emma jumped slightly as Ben re-entered the room. Emma let out a small, nervous laugh and stood, brushing ash and dust from her jeans.

"There's a bed in the back room," Ben said. "You might want to take a shower first," he added, disgust crossing his face again.

Smith shifted uncomfortably and Emma shot Ben a reproachful look.

"A shower will help you get warm," he qualified, lamely.

Smith nodded.

"Thank you," he said, stiffly.

"Down the hall to your right. I left the door open and there are towels on the shelf."

Smith drained the last of his tea and stood slowly, testing his aching legs. He was about to leave the room when Emma stopped him.

"You can leave your jacket here if you'd like. It'll dry faster by the fire."

She seemed to be staring at his chest and after a moment he realised why.

The knife, he thought. The one he kept hidden in the lining of his jacket for emergencies. It was a nasty looking thing; a large bowie knife, covered in nicks and scratches. And probably even a little dried blood.

"No," he said quietly. "No thank you. I prefer to keep everything with me."

"No problem," she said lightly. But her eyes never moved from his chest.

Ben gave him plenty of room as he passed.

Smith closed the door behind him and stood with one ear pressed against it. He didn't have to wait long before they started talking about him.

"What are you doing?" Ben demanded.

"I couldn't just let him leave." Smith could hear the reproach in Emma's voice as she answered.

"And who do you think is going to clean up after your little project?"

Smith smiled and quietly left them to bicker.

Half an hour later, he left the bathroom in a haze of steam. He hadn't wanted to put his old clothes back on, but no one had offered him anything else, so he didn't really have a choice. For a moment he regretted not leaving his clothes to dry with Emma, reasoning that she would have had to offer him something else to wear while they waited. But that would have meant leaving his knives, along with the small pieces of broken glass, sharp bits of tin and trapping equipment along with them. Or worse, it would have meant emptying out his pockets in front of her. Ben was already openly hostile towards him, and even Emma might have reconsidered letting him stay if she had seen what he was carrying around with him. So, he unwillingly pulled his old clothes back on, trying not to wince as the stiffened fabric chafed against his newly scrubbed skin.

As he walked back into the main area of the cabin, Smith could smell something cooking. His mouth began to water and he heard his stomach growl. He tried to remember how long it had been since he'd last eaten a hot meal.

Ben was at the stove in the little kitchen area. Once again, Smith wondered at this naivety in leaving his back turned to a stranger. Especially when they knew that he had a weapon on him. Smith hadn't taken more than two steps before Ben turned around, as if alerted to his presence. He saw the now familiar grimace pass across Ben's face as he locked eyes with him. Ben slowly dropped his gaze to take in Smith's clothes. Without the stink of his own body odour to cover it up, Smith could tell exactly how bad they smelt but he wasn't about to apologise to Ben.

"I hope soup's ok," Ben said breaking the silence.

Smith forced his face into what he hoped was an appropriate mask of gratitude.

"Soup's fine. Thank you."

"The rain's stopped." Ben's tone was deliberately neutral.

Smith listened and realised that Ben was right. The soft pattering against the windows had stopped.

"Yes," he agreed carefully.

"And it's getting late now," Ben continued.

"Where's Emma?" Smith was surprised to find that he was suddenly uneasy without her presence. He scanned the kitchen and noticed that one of the knives was missing from the knife block. It was an effort to keep himself from touching his own knife, still tucked into the lining of his jacket.

"Emma's around." Ben said.

He spotted the knife, lying on the counter next to Ben. He tried to move casually towards it but something in his movement must have given him away. Ben took a single step to his left, effectively blocking his path.

"Where is she?" Smith demanded.

Ben met his gaze again and his eyes were cold.

"You should leave," he said quietly.

The sound of the car door slamming startled them both. A moment later, the cabin door opened, and Emma appeared.

"Oh, good the soup is ready. I'm starving." Her tone was bright. "Oh, I'm sorry, Smith," she continued, contrition plain on her face. "I didn't mean literally 'starving' of course. That was very thoughtless of me. I can make you up a bag of food to take with you tomorrow. Unless you're planning on staying for more than one night?"

Behind him, Ben made a strangled noise. Smith shook his head.

"No? Well then the least we can do is get some hot food into you tonight."

She sauntered over to the table and looked expectantly at Ben.

It seemed obvious to Smith that Emma had money. It wasn't her easy offer to share her food or to let him stay at the cabin – in fact, if anything, that marked her out as being different to typical rich girls – it was in the way she spoke, her expectation that her every suggestion would be obeyed, her general sense of entitlement. Ben on the other hand seemed a bit out of place. He was young and good-looking, but he just wasn't in Emma's league. His clothes were nice but not designer, his hair was nice but obviously not expensively cut. More importantly though he was deferential to Emma. How ever much he disagreed with her decisions tonight, he was never going to argue with her.

No, Smith decided. They're too mismatched to be a 'real' couple. This is just your average case of a spoilt little rich girl coming up to daddy's cabin to screw the gardener.

Idly, he wondered if anybody knew they were up here – and how much money Emma's rich daddy would be willing to part with should she get herself into any trouble.

"Are you finished?" Emma's question interrupted his train of thought.

He looked down at his empty bowl.

"There's some more in the pot. I'll get it for you." She held a hand out for his bowl.

"Don't you want any more?" he asked.

"No, I'm full and Ben has hardly touched his anyway."

96

Smith glanced at Ben's bowl and realised Emma was right.

Ben gave a small sigh and began eating his soup, determinedly, one mouthful after another.

"There you go." Emma placed the bowl back in front of Smith and returned to her seat, watching him with bright eyes from behind her own empty bowl.

Only the rich can afford to go hungry.

Smith finished his second bowl of soup and sat back, contented, in his chair. He could feel the warmth of the meal radiating out from his stomach and spreading through him. He felt pleasantly drowsy, as if he had drunk a glass of whisky with his meal.

Across the table from him, Emma yawned.

"Excuse me," she said, covering her mouth with her hand. "I seem to be tired all of a sudden."

"It's late," Ben pointed out.

She yawned again.

"Yes. If you gentlemen would excuse me I think I'm going to turn in for the night."

"We should probably all go to bed," Ben said, looking meaningfully at Smith.

"Oh yes, Smith, I'm sorry did Ben show you where your room is?" Emma asked.

"Down the hall to the right. I left the door open." The reluctance in Ben's voice was plain.

Smith stood up and stumbled slightly.

"Are you alright?" Emma asked and he nodded.

"Just tired," he said.

He took a tentative step forward, pleased that his legs held him, and pointed his body towards the door.

"Goodnight then," he said awkwardly.

"Sleep well," Emma replied.

Ben said nothing.

Smith found his room and pulled the door closed behind him, breathing a sigh of relief as he did so. He took his jacket off and dumped it beside the bed. His fingers fumbled clumsily with the laces on his boots, and he frowned in frustration as he tried to make them work. After what seemed like an age but was probably only a few minutes, he managed to loosen his boots enough to pull them off.

There was a single framed photograph on the table by the side of the bed and Smith turned it round, peering at it through bleary eyes. It was a picture of what appeared to be a young family – mother, father and two little girls.

Must be Emma and her sister when they were kids. Cute.

Smith replaced the photo, lay down on the bed and fell asleep.

He woke with a bang several hours later. His head hurt and his mouth was dry. He still felt tired, as if his sleep hadn't refreshed him at all, despite the fact that he couldn't remember having woken in the night. Gradually he became aware of a strangeness in his own body, as if he was lying at an awkward angle. He tried to stretch and realised he couldn't move. Panic gripped him as he realised his wrists and ankles were bound. He pulled desperately at his binding and something hard and sharp cut into his skin. Cable ties, he realised.

"There's no point." Ben's voice came out of the darkness, startling him.

"Ben? What's going on?"

Smith heard the sound of a chair scraping slightly on the wooden floorboards and he realised his captor was now standing. A moment later, Ben's face loomed into view above him.

"You should have left when you had the chance."

There was a note of something that almost sounded like regret in Ben's voice. Smith latched onto it.

"I can leave now. Please – I'll go away and I'll never tell anyone about you."

Ben laughed humourlessly.

"Of course you won't. Who would you tell? Who would believe you?"

"Let me go, you sick bastard!" Smith practically screamed.

"Ben?" It was Emma's voice, coming from the doorway. "What's going on in here?"

"Emma!" Smith cried. "Emma, please he's gone crazy."

"He's awake," Ben said, his voice dull.

"I can hear that."

"Emma?" Smith turned it into a question this time.

"I'll be right with you, Smith," she said. "Ben, I think you should go."

"Go?" Ben's voice was incredulous. "But -"

"Shh." She kissed him lightly on the cheek. "You trust me right? You go and warm the car up, I'll take care of this whole mess and then we can go. Ok?"

Smith breathed a sigh of relief as he heard Ben's footsteps retreating.

"Quick," he said urgently. "There's a knife in my jacket."

"This knife?" she held it up.

He blinked.

"That's the one. Use it to cut the ties and then we can both get out of here before he comes back."

She regarded the knife carefully, watching as the light from the rapidly rising sun glinted off the blade. A slow smile spread across her face.

"Why would I want to do that when I took so much trouble to get you here?"

"You? But Ben -"

She laughed.

"Ben's a nice guy but he's never had an original idea in his life. He just does the heavy lifting so to speak."

Smith's guts seemed to twist.

"Why?" he managed.

She laughed.

"Why? Because I can. Because you're here, because no one will miss you, because you were even good enough to bring your own knife." She laughed again. "Why not?"

"You'll get caught. If they find a body at your family's cabin they'll know it was you."

"This isn't my family's cabin. I have no idea whose cabin this is. My family are a much more 'place on the beach' kind of family. As a matter of fact, that's where I am right now. With Ben and five other people who will all swear I was there the whole night."

His heart sank and he felt a single tear run down his cheek.

"Oh, cheer up. Didn't I give you a nice hot meal and a comfortable bed? Didn't I give you the best night you've had in ages? Honestly, some people are just so ungrateful." She grinned down at him, and he wondered how he could possibly have missed the madness lurking behind those perfect blue eyes.

"Anyway, I'll do my best with this next part, but you'll have to be patient with me. I've only done this a couple of times; I don't have a lot of practice yet."

"You don't have to do this. You could still let me go."

"Oh no, I can't do that. What are the chances that I came up here to this stranger's cabin to find you already here? It's serendipitous you see. Like a gift from the gods. I couldn't just let you go." She laughed. "Please don't think too badly of Ben. Poor boy thought we were coming up here to have sex in a stranger's bed, but he knew that wouldn't be happening as soon as he saw you. I'll find some other way to make it up to him."

She flipped the knife in her hands once more and gave him a speculative look.

"I don't suppose you'd like to tell me your name now?"

He shook his head and she shrugged.

"It doesn't really matter. You'll always be 'Smith' to me."

She raised the knife over her head. He shut his eyes.

This story appears here in this form for the first time. An alternative version of it appears in 'Harvey Duckman Presents' Volume 1, published in April 2019.

Cat's Cradle

The first time Alice saw her, she thought the child must have wandered into the wrong classroom by mistake. Children did that sometimes, especially in the age groups that Alice taught.

She had caught sight of movement from the corner of her eye, looked up from the blackboard, smiled her most reassuring smile – and then frozen.

The girl was standing in the corner of the room, and everything about her was out of place, from the flowery dress with its high collar fastened at her throat, to the way her blonde hair had been tortured into ringlets, to the severe expression on her face as she frowned down at her hands.

Alice followed her gaze and realised the girl was playing cat's cradle, weaving the string through her fingers in a series of intricate patterns.

There was more to it than that though, and it took a moment for Alice's brain to catch up with the fact that she was seeing the autumn sunshine streaming through the girl's body, like light through a dirty window; muted and greyish but visible all the same.

Alice let out a small squeal and the chalk she had been holding dropped from her numb fingers, breaking into three pieces as it hit the floor.

The child looked up and made eye contact with Alice, her mouth dropping open and her eyes widening. As Alice continued to stare, the child's expression changed until she was glaring, rage compressing her features. Then, without warning, she stamped one small foot silently on the floor and vanished.

"Miss," one of the girls in the front row said, leaning forward, the urgency in her tone suggesting to Alice that she had been trying to get her attention for some time. "Miss, are you alright?"

Alice allowed her gaze to sweep across the room. Twenty-five eight and nine-year-olds, with normal hair and normal clothes, all solid and opaque as far as she could see, stared back at her with almost identical expressions of confusion on their faces.

Damn.

"I'm fine," Alice said, and her voice sounded wrong to her as she spoke, higher than her normal register and somehow brittle sounding. "Turn to page..." she glanced down, "er, forty-two in your workbooks and answer the questions there."

Amongst the rustle of pages being turned, she clearly heard one boy whisper to another, "The new teacher's mad."

Damn, she thought again, as she tried to calm her racing heart.

By the end of the day, Alice was beginning to wonder whether she really could be going mad. She hadn't seen any sign of the girl since the morning, but she had spent the whole afternoon feeling as though she was being watched. Not the usual sense of standing in front of a class and trying to keep their attention – but an intense feeling of scrutiny that she had never experienced before. She had tried her best to ignore the feeling, but she had struggled to get to half-past three - and she had never been so relieved to dismiss a class when the bell finally rang.

In the moments of quiet after the last of the children's voices had echoed down the hall, Alice lowered herself into the chair behind her desk and looked around the room, half expecting to see the child looking back at her. Everything was reassuringly normal.

"Rough day?" The woman's voice was friendly as it drifted in through the door, but Alice jumped all the same.

"Oh, I'm sorry. I didn't mean to frighten you." Despite her words, the woman laughed a little as she spoke, and her eyes glittered with mirth.

"Sorry, Deb," Alice said. "I didn't see you there."

The older woman eased her way into the room and stopped in front of Alice, looking down at her with an expression of concern plastered onto her face.

"I hear you had a bit of a funny turn earlier," she said. "Is everything alright?"

The dining hall, Alice knew at once. *The kids must have been gossiping about me at lunch. Great.*

"I'm fine," she said. "I had the start of a migraine coming on, that's all. You know how it can make you a bit spacey sometimes."

"Never had one," Deb said promptly, and with such obvious pride in her voice that Alice found herself trying not to bristle.

"Lucky you," she said instead, forcing herself to smile. "I wouldn't recommend it."

"You're sure that's all it was?" Deb frowned again. "I know the first week in a new school can be intimidating."

Alice looked up at the woman towering over her and suddenly felt like a child being lectured by her teacher. She pushed the chair back from the desk and stood up, bringing herself to eye level with her colleague. "I'm sure," she said.

Deb nodded and turned away.

Alice was about to let her go when a thought occurred to her.

"Deb," she said, "the woman who worked here before me. Was she here long?"

"Jenny? Yes, about fifteen years or so, I would say. Until she retired."

"And was she in the same classroom for all that time?"

"I think so." Deb narrowed her eyes. "Why?"

"And she didn't ever say anything about the room? She never complained about it?"

"Not to me, she didn't. Why? Is there something wrong with the classroom?"

Alice faltered and then finally said, "No. Not really. Only that it's a little draughty."

Deb looked disappointed. "Well, it's an old building. All the rooms have their little flaws. I'm sure those big, modern places you did your training in were all much nicer, although I always find them a bit soulless, personally."

Alice stared at her for a moment before she caught herself. "Yes. You're probably right. Anyway," she gestured vaguely at the pile of papers on her desk. "I should get on."

Once she was alone again, Alice let her gaze drift over to the place where she had last seen the child, as a crazy idea started to take root, and the word 'soulless' tumbled through her mind.

She didn't see the girl again for the next two days. On the third day, she thought she saw a shape through the pane of glass in the classroom door as she arrived to open up, but by the time she had fumbled her key into the lock, it was gone. She told herself it was nothing and began to lay out her lesson plans for the day, ignoring the prickling sensation on the nape of her neck.

The girl appeared part way through Alice's history quiz. One moment the corner of the room was empty, and the next there she was, frowning down at her hands again.

The shock was not quite as bad the second time. Alice paused, coughed, said, "Excuse me," and returned to her quiz on 'The Six Wives of Henry VIII', silently thanking her lucky stars that she was so familiar with the material. She was sure that her hands were shaking, but none of the students seemed to notice. When she finally got to the end of the quiz, she risked a quick glance over to the corner, but the girl was gone.

The shock, as it turned out, came later. When she returned from lunch, she found that the bookshelf had been emptied, its contents strewn over the floor. The gaggle of children coming into the room behind her had stopped short when they noticed the mess.

"Who threw all the books on the floor?" one of the boys asked.

"No one threw them," Alice heard herself say. "I left the window open, and the wind must have blown them off the shelf. Can someone give me a hand to tidy this up, please?"

As she shoved the books back onto the shelf, Alice felt her fear start to mutate into something closer to anger.

When the class left for the day, she took a moment to make sure that there was no one within earshot and then she said, firmly, "What you did today is not acceptable. We don't make a mess of the classroom and we certainly don't treat books that way. Do you understand?"

She waited a moment, but there was no response. With a sigh, she gathered her belongings, locked the door, and left.

And in the morning, she opened the door to find the remnants of her favourite coffee cup in a neat pile next to her desk.

Alice wanted to go home. She wanted to run a hot bath, pour herself a glass of something alcoholic, and just relax somewhere where she didn't have to worry about petulant ghosts smashing up her possessions. The pieces of her mug had sat in the bottom of her bin all day, and she had avoided looking at them, just as she had avoided looking at the place where the ghost liked to make its appearance. Alice was starting to get a stiff neck from all the things she was trying to ignore.

So, her desire for home at the forefront of her mind, she allowed a brief and quiet curse-word to slip out when she realised that Adam, the skinny boy who sat on the fourth row, had left without his backpack. She looked down at her watch and decided to give him ten minutes to collect his bag before she left for the night.

When she looked back up, the ghost was there, watching her.

"What do you want?" Alice shrieked, fighting the urge to throw something at it.

"Miss?"

Alice whirled, to find Adam standing behind her.

"Adam, I -" she began, but the boy cut her off.

"She won't answer you, Miss. She can't talk."

"You can see her too?" Something like relief flooded through her.

Adam nodded. "She's my friend. She's teaching me how to do that thing with the string." He frowned. "I think she's sad though. I see her crying sometimes."

Alice turned back to the girl, but she was already gone.

Adam only stayed for a few minutes, but Alice listened to him as he talked about his 'friend'. He wasn't describing a monster, but a child. A scared, hurt child. Shame washed over her as she listened. When he left, trailing his slightly muddy blue and yellow backpack behind him, Alice sank into her chair and waited.

The teacher's car park emptied. The sun dipped low in the sky. The only sound was the caretaker as he moved through the halls - the keys clanking on his belt reminding Alice uncomfortably of Jacob Marley's chains in 'A Christmas Carol'.

Finally, feeling foolish, she spoke to the empty air. "You can come out now. I won't hurt you." After a moment she added, "I'm friends with Adam too."

In the corner, the girl blinked back into existence.

Alice approached her slowly, her palms held out in front of her in what she hoped the ghost would recognise as a non-threatening gesture. As she got closer she could see that Adam had been right. The girl's cheeks were wet, and her eyes were bright with unshed tears.

She didn't look at Alice, but instead she continued to look down as her hands, weaving the string between her fingers and frowning as she did so.

Alice followed her gaze and noted how the string dangled from the girl's fingers and down the length of her body, criss-crossing her legs and torso and reaching down into the ground, almost as if it was tethering her there.

Marley's chains.

In a flash, Alice understood and, without thinking, she reached for the string. It stayed solid beneath her fingers, and she began to pull on it, wrenching it free from the earth and unwinding it from around the child's body.

The girl closed her fists around the string, clinging to the ruined pattern and opening her mouth in a silent 'o' as if in protest.

Alice dropped to her knees so that she was looking directly into the girl's pale eyes.

"You have to let go," she said, as gently as she could. "Trust me."

For a moment, it seemed to Alice as though the girl was going to refuse, but then she nodded her head, just once, and let go.

Alice pulled the string free and let it drop to the ground. There was a flash of brilliant, white light, and she buried her face in her hands, shielding her eyes. As if from far away, she thought she heard a child laughing.

When she opened her eyes, the room was empty, and there was no sense, this time, of being watched.

The girl was gone.

A Birthday Message

No one should be alone on their birthday. And some
people are - deeply, truly alone. It wasn't as if I had no
friends in the city – Kate had gone out of her way to make
me feel included with her crowd, to throw me the best
party that she could under the circumstances. It's just
that eventually the barman called last orders, the music
stopped, and I knew that I would have to go home to my
silent, empty house.

Kate rode back in the taxi with me, despite the fact
that she lived closer to the bar, and it would have made
more sense to do the two-stage drop-off the other way
around.

"Do you want me to come in with you?" she asked as
we pulled up.

The light in the living room was on a timer, so the
house looked more welcoming than ominous, but I found
that I still didn't want to go inside.

"Or you could come back to mine?" Kate continued.
"Stay over if you like, Dave won't mind."

"I'm fine," I told her. "Thanks for the drinks."

We hugged awkwardly in the small space, and she
wished me happy birthday again, before I scrambled out
of the taxi, bottle bags and a purse hanging from my right

wrist, an oversized helium balloon clutched in my left hand.

Kate must have made the driver wait until I was inside before he left, because I heard the screech of tires as I closed the door behind me. I dumped my stuff in the hallway, leaving the balloon to float off somewhere, before I stepped out of my heels with a sigh.

"I'm officially too old for you," I said ruefully as I kicked them to one side.

Straight away I wished I hadn't spoken. The sound of my voice only seemed to magnify the silence in the rest of the house. I picked up a bottle of wine from one of the bags and limped through to the living room. I cleared a space on the sofa and then spent a few moments digging through the mess on the coffee table until I found the TV remote. The TV flicked on; still set to the same music channel I had been watching before I left for work. Relief flooded through me as the music drove out the silence.

The wine forgotten, I leaned back on the sofa and, with the bubble-gum pop music still blaring in my ears, I fell instantly and deeply asleep.

I woke sometime after ten o'clock on my birthday proper, cracking one eyelid open in an experimental fashion to test how bad the hangover was going to be.

I wasn't terrible. In fact, it was a damn sight better than I had any right to expect given how much I'd had to drink the night before. I reckoned that a cup of tea, a bacon butty and a couple of paracetamol should sort me right out – and then I immediately began to wish that there was somebody here to provide me with the tea and the bacon butty. Maybe I should have stayed over at

Kate's after all? Dave, her lovely and patient husband, would happily have provided us both with strong, builder's tea with too much sugar and all the greasy bacon we could manage. Just the thought of it made me smile.

The smile slipped from my face as I contemplated my own empty house. With an effort, I heaved myself off the sofa and into the kitchen to put the kettle on.

Half an hour later, I was starting to feel better. I'd drunk my tea, eaten my bacon (grilled because I couldn't face standing over a frying pan, but bacon is bacon after all), and taken a couple of painkillers. I'd even put some more music on – quietly – in the background.

And then my phone buzzed – a Facebook notification. I opened it to find that I had three heartfelt 'happy birthday' messages, two memes about getting older, and there - right smack in the middle of my timeline – a Facebook memory from two years ago, complete with a picture of me and Jake.

Fucking Jake.

I'd thought that I had purged myself of his online presence at around the same time that I threw away our wedding photographs, but I must have missed one – and this was the picture that Facebook decided to throw at me on the morning of my fortieth birthday. A picture of the two of us on the last-minute break that he had booked as a surprise for my thirty-eighth birthday. The photograph showed me grinning like an idiot.

I had been an idiot.

One year, eleven months and five days after that picture was taken, my mother died – just before my thirty-ninth birthday. Six days after that my husband confessed all about the affair he had been having with the woman at work. And then, he left me.

I hadn't seen it coming.

"That absolute psycho!" Kate had screamed when I told her. "Who does something like that?"

I had just shrugged, too mired in misery to react.

"Have you seen him since?" she asked.

I shook my head.

"And have you seen …?" she tailed off as I shook my head again, my eyes filling with tears.

"You will," she said. "It just takes a while sometimes."

I clung to the certainty in her voice.

I remembered all of this as I stood at my kitchen table, phone in hand, bacon grease congealing on my plate. And it was enough to spur me into action.

I ran the water until it was scalding hot, then I gathered up every mug, plate, and piece of cutlery in the kitchen and ran them under the tap, washing the worst of the hardened food off them before I chucked them haphazardly into the dishwasher. Then I managed to seal the bin bag that was close to overflowing in the kitchen bin, and to drag it to the wheelie bin waiting outside.

With the kitchen more or less taken care of, I turned my attention to the living room, stuffing most of the contents of the sofa and the coffee table into another bin bag – and then pausing to rescue the TV remote and my spare phone charger before I threw it all away.

I managed what my mum would have called 'a quick run round' with the vacuum cleaner, and then I stopped, breathless, to take stock.

It looked okay. Messy still, but 'lived-in messy' rather than 'desperately unhappy messy'. It was a start, I decided.

And then I heard movement from behind me and I half turned just as a voice said, "Happy birthday, darling."

My mother's voice made me jump. *Just in time*, I thought. I didn't want her to know how lost I had been without her; I didn't want her to worry.

"Mum! How long have you been standing there?"

When I looked closer, I realised that she wasn't so much 'standing' as she was 'floating', her feet vanishing into the top of the coffee table. I made a move to clear it out of her way, before I caught sight of the small frown on her face and remembered, just in time, how much she hated it whenever anyone 'made a fuss' over her new, spectral form. Instead, I plopped down on my newly clean sofa, and gestured for her to join me.

She smiled as she arranged herself, hovering just above the cushions, close enough that she looked like she was really sitting. She must have been practicing the trick for some time because I could tell from the satisfied expression on her face that she was enjoying showing it off.

"Your grandma sends her love," she said, tucking her legs underneath her to complete the illusion. "She wanted to come but you know how she is about travel."

I nodded. Grandma Iris had never even been comfortable taking the number four bus into town, so I wasn't surprised that she hadn't taken the trip from the astral plane.

None of us had known though, when she passed over, whether she didn't come back because she didn't want to travel or because she couldn't travel back to see us. Not everybody could travel back – and none of the experts had been able to explain why.

According to my mum, grandma Iris was having a fine old time in her afterlife, and she was happy to stay there. I didn't begrudge her it – but I did wish that I had known it was her choice before mum died. Maybe that way I wouldn't have worried so much about whether mum would be able to travel back.

"Give her my love," I said, and then, "I'm really glad you're here, mum. Was the traffic bad?"

My mother wrinkled her nose. "Oh, no worse than usual, I suppose," she said as if she was discussing the A1 motorway instead of the link to the great beyond. "Although I swear the queues get longer every time I make the trip." She reached out and laid her hand over mine. I couldn't feel it, but I appreciated the gesture. "Although it was worth it to see you on your special day," she said, smiling.

Gosfeld

The Baker was the first to die.

A bought of coughing overtook him as he tried to sell leftover bread to the children of the village. Cerryn's face twisted in disgust as she watched him splutter over his trays. Finally, he lifted a hand to his mouth – only to have it come away bloody.

Cerryn's eyes widened as she took a step back.

The Baker looked at his shaking hand.

"Wait," he said.

Cerryn took another step, grabbing for Jobin's hand.

"Wait," the man began again, his bloodied palm raised imploringly towards them. "Please wait."

Cerryn shook her head wordlessly and began to back away, dragging Jobin with her. The man took a step forward and Cerryn let out a small, shrill cry as she turned and ran.

The Baker watched as the children scattered. Slowly, he slumped to the ground, sat down amongst his discarded trays, and hid his face in his hands. Waiting.

"Meara!" Jobin hammered on the door to the old apothecary's treatment room. Cerryn added her voice to his and after a moment the door opened. The anger on Meara's face vanished as she took in the children's expressions.

"What's happened?"

"The Baker is coughing up blood." Cerryn told her shortly.

Meara paled.

"Did he touch you? Did he get any blood on you?"

The children shook their heads.

"You're sure?" she asked, grabbing Jobin roughly by the shoulders and manoeuvring him into the light streaming in through the window.

"Ow," he protested.

Meara scrutinised him for a moment before releasing him and turning her attention to Cerryn. The older girl regarded her calmly.

"He didn't touch us. He didn't cough on us. I got Jobin away from him as soon as I saw the blood." There was a trace of pride in her voice as she spoke.

Meara nodded.

"Well done," she said. "I'll need to go to him immediately. Cerryn, finish up with Annie." She indicated the wide-eyed young woman sitting silently in the treatment room. "She needs a simple poultice, nothing more."

"What about me?" Jobin asked.

"Speak to anyone who bought bread today and tell them to throw it away."

Jobin frowned.

"They won't listen."

"Tell them anyway." Meara had already turned away from the children and begun throwing herbs and powders into her pack.

It was late when Meara returned, her boots dragging in the dust.

Jobin crept onto the landing, trying to hold his breath in case his aunt and sister heard him and sent him back to bed.

"How many?" he heard Cerryn ask.

Meara sighed and ran a hand through her greying hair.

"One for now. More will follow."

"Is it ... natural?"

Meara's head snapped up and she glared at Cerryn before dropping her gaze again.

"I don't know yet," she admitted. "There appear to be no marks on the body. If there are other symptoms, there wasn't enough time for me to study them."

Jobin missed his sister's next words, but he was watching Meara's face when she spoke again.

"If it is not natural, we will know soon enough."

Over the next few days, Meara was barely at home. She returned only to eat and rest briefly before replenishing her herbs and heading back out into the village.

"Won't you let me come with you?" Cerryn asked her. "I could help."

"This is beyond your capabilities," Meara snapped. "For the moment," she added, as Cerryn's face dropped. "Stay here. Make sure we have enough wolfsbane and heartroot powder. Treat anyone who comes to the door as best you can – as long as they're not showing any symptoms of the disease." She raised a finger in Cerryn's face, as if to underscore the seriousness of her words. "If you suspect they have the sickness, you turn them away."

"Meara!" Jobin almost winced at the shock in his sister's voice. "We're healers. We took an oath."

"I took an oath, not you. You're still a child. And besides," she said, her face softening. "You can't help anyone if you get sick yourself."

After a moment, Cerryn nodded slowly.

"You should rest," she said quietly. "I'll wake you if anyone comes to the door."

Jobin thought Meara would argue, but to his surprise she nodded, once, curtly, and curled up on the armchair. He dragged a woollen blanket over her thin frame and her lips quirked upwards in a quick smile. Despite the fact that she hadn't opened her eyes, he smiled back before he tiptoed away and sunk silently into the chair opposite her.

A pounding at the door woke him soon after. Startled, he was on his feet before he realised what was happening.

"What is it?" Cerryn asked, as she opened the door.

"I need to see her. Now."

"She's sleeping." Jobin could hear the reproach in Cerryn's voice.

"It's all right, Cerryn." Meara stood, wiping her eyes with the back of her hand. "Well," she demanded. "What is it?"

"Your presence is required," the man said.

"Very well." Meara turned to pick up her bag.

"You won't need that," he said. "Eoin has called a village meeting. He wants you there."

Meara's eyes narrowed.

"And does Eoin understand the manner in which a sickness such as this one can spread? No -" she held up a hand to cut him off as he attempted to respond. "I will ask him myself." Pointedly, she picked up the bag and held it inches from his face. "And I will almost certainly need this."

Jobin and Cerryn stared wordlessly at one another as Meara left, slamming the door behind her.

Jobin had no trouble finding the meeting. Even if it hadn't been virtually the only light source in the entire village, he would have been able to hear the shouting long before he got there. Meara was standing at the front of the room, next to a tall blond man who Jobin recognised as Eoin. Somehow, despite the difference in their sizes and the fact that she had been summoned to the meeting, it appeared to Jobin that Meara was the one holding court and that Eoin was merely waiting on her.

"One at a time!" Eoin was shouting. "Friends, please. One at a time!"

"We must send word to Verrine!" a woman shouted. The crowd roared in agreement.

"Verrine will not help us." Meara's voice cut through the noise of the gathered villagers.

"We're worth something to them, surely?" asked Eoin, when the noise had died down enough for him to make himself heard again.

She snorted.

"As what? If Gosfeld ceases to exist they will find someone else to supply them. Or do you suppose we are the only village with nets and boats?"

The noise rose again. Jobin had seen enough. Meara was convinced that no help was coming. Quietly, he left the way he had come in.

The fog rolled in the next day.

Jobin looked out into the street and was met with a wall of white, so thick that he could barely make out the houses opposite his own. There was a strange cast to the shadows, as though the fog had made everything unstable, as though at any moment the houses might tumble into view and crush him as he stood at the window. Shivering, Jobin turned away.

They saw no one for days. Nobody came to the door, nobody called out to them from the street. It was as though the ever-present white fog had made everyone too afraid to travel.

"Does that mean that the sickness is over?" Jobin asked.

Meara and Cerryn exchanged glances, and he saw the meaning behind their eyes.

Later, in his room, he racked his brains to try to remember every story he had ever heard about magical sickness. There were the stories of revenge curses, sent by powerful wizards, and Jobin shuddered as he wondered who, in Gosfeld, could have incurred the wrath of a wizard. Then there were the stories about demon-made sicknesses that wiped out entire towns without leaving a single survivor to tell the tale. *Although*, he reasoned, *someone must have been able to tell the tale.* Jobin couldn't remember hearing any stories about a sickness that was accompanied by fog and, the more he thought about it, the more he decided that he would have to go outside and get a proper look at it.

He waited until he heard first Cerryn and then Meara go to bed. Then he waited a little longer, just to be certain. Quietly, he slipped out of bed and made his way to the window, holding his breath the whole time. The drop from his window to the street below was not a long one and Jobin knew from experience that there was very little chance of him getting hurt, but the thought of the hard ground below him was not what made his palms sweat and his breathing become ragged. Shakily, he climbed onto the sill and, taking a deep breath, dropped to the street.

He hit the ground with a muffled thud. Pausing, he looked around, but he couldn't see more than a few feet in front of him. He shivered. The fog was cold – that much he had expected – but it was a strange kind of coldness, one that seemed to envelop him and leach the heat right out of his bones. Rubbing his hands together, he took a few steps forward and then stopped. The streets were silent. In the whole of his young life, Jobin had never known the village to be silent. There was always the sound of dogs barking, songs being sung in the tavern, couples arguing - but tonight he couldn't hear a thing.

As the silence stretched, Jobin became aware of the strange feeling that something was watching him. He was reminded of a game he used to play as a young boy, where all the children in the village would make believe that the last one home would be snatched away by demons – laughing and whooping as they raced each other through the streets. Some small part of Jobin had always felt a prickle of fear that he might be slower than the rest - that he really might be taken by the demons - even as he'd plastered a grin over his face. Tonight though, there was no fun – just an unnerving sense of something dangerous lurking in the streets. Fear bubbled up in Jobin's chest and he ran the few steps back to his house, threw himself clumsily at the window and hauled himself over the sill, landing in a heap on the floor. Wide-eyed and panting, he scrambled away from the window, expecting that at any moment something might follow him into the room. Long minutes passed while

Jobin's breathing returned to normal and his heart started to slow. Nothing came through. Nothing followed him. He was alone.

Slowly, he climbed to his feet and crept to the door, half expecting that his fall would have woken Cerryn. He eased the door open and moved quietly into the hall outside her room. Cerryn's door was open and Jobin froze, certain she would be awake.

"Sorry," he said quietly.

Cerryn didn't stir.

"Cerryn?" he whispered. "Are you awake?"

Jobin crept forward until he was standing just outside her room. Even from a distance he could see that her face was pale and covered in a light sheen of sweat. He gasped and tried to call out for Meara, but fear had stolen his voice. Shaking his head, as if to banish the sight of his sister from his mind, he stumbled away to find help.

Although she wouldn't let him help her, Meara had not tried to banish Jobin from Cerryn's side. They spent most of the day in silence, watching the slow rise and fall of her chest as she lay, almost motionless in the bed.

"There are stories," he began hesitantly. "About the sickness."

"Stories are very different from the reality."

"I have seen the reality," he snapped.

Meara's face softened.

"So you have," she agreed.

After a moment, he continued.

"The stories say that the sickness was created by a monster. And that the Order of Shandere drove the monster away. Shouldn't we -"

Before Jobin could finish speaking, Meara was in front of him. Quicker than he would have thought possible, she leapt from her stool and crossed the room. She gripped him by the shoulders, her face inches from his own.

"Listen to me, Jobin. This is not a story. The Order are not going to ride into Gosfeld and save the day."

"But they -"

"No. Believe me when I tell you that it is far too dangerous to go looking for them." She sighed heavily, gazing at Cerryn's prone form. "I'm afraid we are on our own."

Jobin paced the floor in his room. A fire seemed to burn in his chest as he considered Meara's words. *We're on our own. I'm afraid we are on our own.* The words seemed to echo in his mind. *They're right there!* he wanted to scream at her. *The Order are right outside Verrine and you want to stay here and do nothing while Cerryn dies!* His eyes watered and he scrubbed at them furiously with the back of his hand. *Then you stay. Stay here and be damned! I'm going to go find someone who can actually help us!*

It was late when he left. He'd taken some dried meat from the pantry when he had prepared Meara's supper and he had thought about taking some of her herbs to try to protect himself from the sickness while he travelled. Cerryn would have known what he should take, but as Jobin read the names, scrawled in Meara's tiny handwriting, he realised that it was all meaningless to him. Sighing, he had replaced the jars carefully on her shelf and added a handful of dried fruit to his small pack. It was at least a day's ride to Verrine, and he didn't want to go hungry.

The road to Verrine was dangerous, he knew. Everyone had heard the stories of the Raiders that lived in the woods, preying on merchants and unfortunate travellers who strayed too close to their lands. Although Gosfeld had largely been spared the worst of their attentions in Jobin's lifetime, he had heard some of the older men tell tales that made his stomach tighten. He tried to put the stories out of his mind as he crept towards the stables. It took all his concentration to find his way through the thick, white fog. Just when Jobin was beginning to think that he had taken a wrong turn somewhere, he was rewarded with the sound of a muffled whinny. Silently thanking whichever gods had been looking out for him, Jobin lifted the bar across the stable doors and heaved them open. Inside it was dark but there was none of the strange clamminess that was starting to permeate the streets outside. He could hear the horses moving restlessly and smell the strangely sweet smell of horse-hair and hay. Jobin moved quickly down the stalls until he found the horse he was looking for: a brown mare.

"Hey girl," he said quietly, in what he hoped was a soothing tone. He held his hand out and after a moment she moved forward and sniffed it. When she didn't bite or make any unexpected sounds, he decided that he should be safe to bring her out of the stall. Moving carefully, so that he didn't spook her, Jobin saddled the mare and led her outside.

By the time they had cleared the outskirts of the village, the fog had lifted, giving way to a cold, clear night. Jobin stared wonderingly up at the moon. It had been days since he had been able to see the sky and the waxing moon seemed to him to be as bright at the afternoon sun. With a final glance back in the direction of his home, Jobin pulled himself up into the saddle and nudged the mare onto the path and in the direction of Verrine.

It was almost first light by the time Jobin reached the forest. He felt the mare tense underneath him and reached a hand down to stroke her neck, making shushing sounds as he did so. Inside he could see that the dense trees were blocking most of the weak sunlight and it took every ounce of his courage not to turn around and go back. The stories he had heard about the Raiders almost always took place in the forest, and Meara had warned him all the time when he was a child never to go near the place. Straining his ears, he could hear nothing except for the sounds of birds singing their dawn chorus. Gently, he eased his horse forwards.

Jobin was deep into the forest when he smelt it; a kind of burnt meat smell. Grimacing, he tried to place what kind of meat it could be. It seemed to him that there was something wrong with it, something strange about the smell of it. Distracted, he didn't notice the object hanging from the tree until he was right underneath it. He frowned and brought the horse to a standstill so that he could get a closer look. Bile rose in his throat as he recognised the object hanging from the tree like some kind of bizarre trophy – a human skull.

A sound like high pitched laughter rang out. He froze, holding his breath.

Maybe it was a bird?

The horse shifted uncomfortably underneath him, her ears starting to flatten against her skull. Behind them Jobin heard the cracking of twigs on the path, and then that strange laughing sound again. The horse started to turn in the direction of the sound and Jobin instinctively pulled the reigns, hauling her back onto the path. Out of the corner of his eye, Jobin was aware of movement in the trees. In a rush, he let out the breath he had been holding, and kicked the horse's flank, urging her into a run.

Branches whipped past his face as they ran. The noises behind him had intensified – the laughter being joined by shouting and whooping – and all of it was almost drowned out by the pounding of the blood in his ears. Suddenly, Jobin was aware of the saddle slipping beneath him. He realised immediately that he hadn't fastened it tight enough around the mare's stomach. Dropping the reigns, he tried to throw his arms around her neck, just as the saddle slid to the right. He lost his grip and, with a cry of despair, he fell, landing heavily on the path below. Winded, he managed to force himself to roll off the path and into the bushes as the mare galloped away.

Jobin pulled his cloak tightly around himself and squeezed his eyes shut as he tried to draw breath into his aching lungs. He could hear the sounds of footsteps and shouting - and he was convinced with every second that passed that someone would reach down and drag him from the bushes. But nobody did. It felt like hours before the forest became quiet again. Finally, Jobin crawled out from under the bush and climbed shakily to his feet.

Keeping to the undergrowth he limped alongside the path.

He spent the rest of the day limping towards Verrine. Twice more he thought he heard the sounds of people moving through the trees around him, and each time he threw himself into the bushes and prayed to whatever gods might be listening that the Raiders didn't find him. Finally, the sun sunk so low that he couldn't continue making his way through the undergrowth. For the first time in hours, he stopped to consider his position.

Stay here and rest for the night, or risk walking the rest of the way on the path?

The idea of walking in the open made Jobin shiver, but the idea of spending the night in the forest - and of delaying his arrival in Verrine - seemed to him to be even worse. Cautiously, he crawled out of the undergrowth and made his way slowly along the path.

He had been walking for only a few minutes before he realised that he was close to the edge of the woods. Up ahead he could see that the trees were thinning out, and, beyond the ever-present gloom of the woods, the sky was still a pale silvery grey – the last of the daylight holding fast against the approaching darkness.

For the first time in days, Jobin felt something like hope rise up inside him. He could make it out of the forest before nightfall! He could make it to Verrine! He could -

Snap.

Jobin whirled at the sound. There, on the path behind him, was a tall, skinny figure. Despite the fact that he couldn't see its face, Jobin had the uncanny impression that it was baring its teeth at him. He took a step backwards. The figure took a single step forwards, almost as if it was mocking him. That wild, chittering laugh sounded again and Jobin lost his nerve entirely, turned, and ran.

His aches and pains forgotten, Jobin ran as fast as he could, arms and legs pumping as he tried desperately to outrun the thing on the path behind him. He stumbled – once, twice – and then caught himself just before he lost his balance entirely. His blood was loud in his ears but even over the sound of it, he could hear the Raiders' wild laughter, their inhuman, wordless cries. He could almost feel the heat on his back from the Raider behind him, could almost sense a clawed hand reaching out to grasp him. A scream rose in Jobin's throat, and he choked it down as he headed towards the lights.

He burst through the tree-line, just as the figure threw himself into a tackle. Jobin and the Raider fell in a tangled heap of limbs.

"Get off me! Get off!" he screamed, kicking out desperately. Through tear-blurred eyes, he could see the lights of the camp before him and the thought of failing now, when he had come so far, made Jobin frantic. With an animal cry that could almost have matched the Raiders' own, he kicked out with both legs and was rewarded with a satisfying crunch and a howl of pain. The man rolled away, clutching at his face and Jobin could see the blood running between his fingers. He had no time to catch his breath before more of the figures began swarming out of the forest. Ignoring their fallen comrade, they came straight for Jobin, who scrambled to his feet and ran. He could feel them gaining on him and he let out the last of the air in his lungs in a despairing cry that split the night.

There – silhouetted against the light from the camp – was a horse and rider, headed towards them. With the last of his energy, Jobin threw himself from the path, and the horse thundered past him. He curled up in the grass and tried to ignore the screams. It didn't take long for silence to be restored. When Jobin opened his eyes, he found a man bending over him, suspicion etched into his features, and the insignia of the Order of Shandere bright against his dark tunic.

"Please," Jobin rasped. "Help."

There was a long pause before the man reached down and hauled Jobin to his feet.

"Come on, lad," he said, shortly. "You'll ride with me. Caleb will want to speak to you."

Jobin gulped gratefully at the beaker of water. In the fading light, it seemed to have a strange blue tint to it, but it tasted fine, and he was glad of its soothing effect on his throat.

"Does your village have an apothecary? A healer?"

"Only Meara. But she hasn't been able to stop the sickness."

"Interesting. Did she send you to find us?"

Jobin shook his head. "No." Almost against his will he added; "Actually she told me not to look for you."

"Did she give you a reason?"

"She said it was too dangerous."

"And yet you came anyway." He bent down and regarded Jobin closely. "I wonder if that speaks more to your lack of discipline or to the strength of your faith."

The taller man snorted.

"It probably speaks more to his desperation. Look at him, Caleb. The boy can barely stand."

Abruptly, Caleb straightened.

"Take him inside. Give him more to drink and check him for marks. Report back to me once that is done. I will make a decision then."

"What are you looking for?"

"The mark," the soldier answered brusquely.

Jobin shivered.

"What's that?"

"It's a sign on your body. Something that tells me whether you've been infected."

"There are no marks," Jobin said, remembering what he'd overheard. "Meara and Cerryn said so."

"Is that right? And what would they know about it?"

"Meara is our healer."

"And the other girl? Cerryn?"

"She's training to be a healer like Meara. And she's my sister." Jobin choked back a sob. "And she's sick."

The man went very still for a moment. When he spoke again, his tone was almost gentle.

"Perhaps there are marks and your healers lack the training to recognise them. I mean no disrespect to your loved ones," he said quickly, before Jobin could argue. "I wouldn't expect a village healer to have much experience with something like this. That is why you came to us, after all."

Jobin nodded slowly.

"Right then." He patted Jobin lightly on the shoulder. "No marks. You can get dressed now."

Jobin reached for his discarded clothes, but the man stopped him.

"No, boy. Put these on instead." He handed Jobin a white tunic and pants. "I'll have someone burn these old things."

He dressed quickly. The tunic was cut tight at the neck, and he pulled at it self-consciously.

"Now," the man said, handing Jobin another glass of the pale, blue liquid. "Is there anything else you think we might need to know?"

"... can be no doubt?" Half waking, Jobin recognised Caleb's voice.

"None at all."

A sigh.

"Very well then. We ride at first light."

"And the boy?"

A pause.

"He is clean?" Caleb asked.

"He is unmarked."

"Bring him with us."

Jobin heard a rustle of fabric and then sleep drew him back under again.

As they approached the edge of the forest, Jobin saw the figure of the Raider, still lying where he had left him. Caleb dismounted and nudged the dead man with his foot, so that his body rolled over and lay face up. In the light of day, Jobin saw that he did not possess the monstrous features he had imagined. He was just a man. A dirty, bloodied man.

"Raider," Caleb said. "It looks like he's been clubbed to death."

"But," stammered Jobin, "He was alive."

"You didn't do this, boy," Caleb told him. "The other Raiders did."

He spat on the ground next to the Raider's body.

"Animals," he said.

On horseback and sticking to the path, the riders made their way quickly through the forest. Jobin didn't see or hear any signs of the Raiders, although he pulled his cloak over his nose and mouth to block out the smell of burnt meant, and he closed his eyes as they passed the place where the skull still hung from the tree.

Caleb gave the order to dismount just outside Gosfeld. Jobin watched as the men went efficiently about their tasks, preparing armour, lighting torches, organising into groups. No one paid any attention to the small boy in their midst and, when they moved into the village, no one noticed that he had already gone.

Making his way through the streets towards his home, Jobin saw movement out of the corner of his eye. He swung around just in time to see a shadow shuffling away from him through the streets.

"Hey!" he shouted, his voice strangely muffled.

The thing didn't stop.

He was about to give chase when he noticed a second shadow nearby. As he turned towards it, he heard a low growl cut through the strange soundlessness. Before he could take a step, the thing was somehow closer to him – although Jobin couldn't be sure whether it had moved or whether it had grown to fill the space between them. He edged backwards until his back hit a wall. And still the thing seemed to flow towards him, filling his whole vision with its blank, featureless blackness.

It growled again, a low rumbling sound that seemed to echo all around them. Jobin felt his entire body go cold, and he fought for breath as his world started to fade to black. He felt his legs give out underneath him, felt the stones of the wall behind him scrape along his back as he crumpled to the ground. He closed his eyes.

"Get back!" Jobin recognised Meara's voice. With an effort, he dragged his eyes back open just in time to watch her fling something in the direction of the shadow. He heard a noise like a wounded animal, and the thing retreated, seeming to shrink into itself.

"What did you ... what did you do?" Talking was an effort.

"Drove it away. But it will be back." She leaned down and pulled him to his feet. "You must get to safety before it returns."

"I brought ..."

"The Order of Shandere. I know." She frowned. "I warned you not to go to them. And now you have no choice but to return to them." She turned away.

"You're not coming with me?"

Meara drew in a deep, shaky breath.

"When Caleb asks you what you saw here, do not speak of the shadow." She paused. "And do not drink the blue water."

Caleb marched forward when he saw Jobin reappear from the fog.

"You shouldn't have run off like that." Despite his measured tone, the anger was clear on his face.

"I'm sorry. I had to try to find my sister."

"And did you?"

Jobin shook his head.

"I got lost in the fog,"

"Tell me then, what did you see in there?"

"Nothing, sir."

"Nothing?"

"Just ... just the fog."

Caleb stared at him for a long moment but said nothing. After a moment, he turned to the old soldier.

"He is clean." The man said. "His faith is strong."

Caleb sighed.

"Are there any others?"

The man shrugged.

"Perhaps. There are other children here. Their innocence may have protected them."

"Very well. Separate the children and test them. We will take the boys."

"And the girls?"

"Take them to Verrine."

Caleb turned to Jobin.

"This witch of yours. The 'healer'. Did you see her in there?"

Jobin shook his head.

Caleb turned back to the soldier.

"She's likely fled by now but see if you can find her."

"And the rest?"

"There's nothing to be done for them. They have all seen the demons."

Jobin felt his heart drop into the pit of his stomach as Caleb beckoned the torchbearers forward and indicated the village.

"Cleanse them," he said.

This story first appeared in 'Harvey Duckman Presents' Volume 3, published in October 2019.

Soundproof

"Don't be fooled." The woman said, nodding towards the small figure huddled in the cell. "It might be small, but it's lethal. Its power lies in communication, but the glass is soundproof, and we've disabled the intercom so you're not in any danger. First time down here?"

"Yes."

"You get used to it after a while." She studied him, unsmiling. "Have a good shift."

He mumbled something incoherent in return, as he did his best to suppress a shudder.

He'd heard the stories in basic training, of course; whole units who went crazy and turned on each other, or worse, killed the civilians they'd been assigned to protect. There were things he'd seen at the academy - recordings, photographs - things he still couldn't think about without feeling the bile start to creep up his throat.

The last of the scientists left around three. Just headed back out into the world as if they didn't know about the things that were really out there. Alone, he stepped closer to the glass and peered through. The thing inside was small and as he watched it rolled over and unfurled itself, almost as if it had waited to get a better look at him too. He took a step back, hand tightening on his gun. The thing looked like a child. Not a demonic approximation of a child, not a horror movie child - there were no pitch-black eyes or impossibly flexible limbs - just a totally normal kid. Somehow, that was so much worse than anything he'd been expecting.

Six a.m. He trudged up the last flight of stairs and grimaced at the lights in the control room, too bright after the dim emergency lighting in the tunnels.

"You off?" It was Roth. He'd recognised Roth on his first day, remembered seeing him around the academy and he'd been pleased to see - if not a friendly face, exactly, then at least a familiar one.

"Yeah," he said now, too tired for small talk.

"Me too. Fancy a drink?"

"At six in the morning?"

Roth snorted. "You can get anything round here, mate, if you know where to look. Come on."

He hesitated but only for a second. The images were still playing somewhere in the back of his mind. Maybe a quick beer would help him sleep.

The place was a dive, but that was no great surprise. Roth swung himself onto the bar stool with practiced ease and held up two fingers.

The barman nodded and slid two bottles down the bar towards them.

"Cheers," Roth said, tipping the neck of his bottle towards him. "You survived your first night."

He picked up the second bottle and took a swig. Warm, off-brand beer but it would do.

"Did you see it then?" Roth asked.

"The ... demon?" he felt stupid saying it, but if Roth thought there was anything funny he didn't react.

"Yeah, did you get a good look at it?"

"It looks ..." he hesitated.

"Like a kid, right?" Roth pressed. "Exactly like a kid."

He nodded, beer bottle pressed against his lips, pretending to drink so he didn't have to speak.

"Ever wonder how the extraction teams know what to take and what to leave behind?"

There was a kind of glee in Roth's voice now, and part of him wanted to stop this conversation in its tracks, make his excuses and leave, but a bigger part of him wanted to know what Roth knew.

Roth didn't wait for him to ask. "They don't know. There's no way to tell the demon from an actual kid. They have to wait until something happens, some kind of event that fits the profile - something like Jonestown say, or Salem - and then they go in and retrieve whatever's left."

"Wait. Jonestown?"

"More than likely. Fits the pattern."

"But, Salem?"

Roth finished his beer in one long, noisy slurp. "Been here for centuries, mate. Course, we'll never really know for sure, will we. Another beer?"

He shook his head. "I better not. I'm going to head off, try to get some sleep before my next shift."

Roth laughed humourlessly. "Good luck with that."

The next night, he thought the thing looked different. He stared at it, trying to figure out what had changed. Maybe it was taller? Skinnier? There was definitely something different about it, some small change. He heard footsteps coming up the tunnel and he turned away, pretended he hadn't been looking. When he checked back later, it was different again.

He was almost eager to be alone with it after that, eager to figure out what was different. There was something like an itch at the back of his brain, as if he'd been given some piece of information that he couldn't quite put together. As he watched, it tilted its head to one side, adopting an expression of curiosity and then reached out a hand and beckoned.

He stepped forward, stopping just short of the glass. The thing opened its mouth and he half smiled.

"It's no good," he said. "I can't hear you."

The thing stuck out its lower lip in an uncanny imitation of a petulant child.

"Have you ever thought," Roth asked, falling into step with him, "about how they justify the cost?"

"Cost?" He felt slow and stupid this morning. It was his fourth overnight shift, his fourth morning following Roth to the bar, and his thoughts felt like mud clogging his brain. "I guess they lie to the taxpayers, same as every other government."

"Not that cost." Roth was staring at him, with eyes that seemed to burn too brightly in his pale face. "The human cost. Think about it, they send a team of people in to collect a thing that can literally talk you to death. How many people die, do you reckon, each time they bring one of those things in?"

"I don't -"

"Five people? Fifty? And for what? Intel? How are we going to get intel from something if we can't listen to it?"

"Maybe they just want it off the streets." His voice sounded flat even to himself.

"Yeah, I'm sure the higher-ups have some grand plan." Roth performed a parody of a salute.

He sighed.

The tunnels were busy. There were new faces, all of them in lab coats and all of them moving quickly. He radioed up to Roth.

"Something happening?" he asked.

"Things are going to get a little lively around here tonight. They're bringing in a new extraction. Sit tight, kid, and keep your eyes open."

Behind the glass the demon was changing shape again – skin colour, hair colour, height – so quickly that he could hardly follow it. Something about it made him think of an insect beating its wings against glass. He turned away.

He almost didn't notice the activity trailing off until it was abruptly quiet. He looked up to find the demon had stopped changing shape and had settled on the form it had been wearing the first time he saw it.

He shook his head, and was just about to resume his position, when the radio at his side flared into life with a loud hiss of static.

"Say again," he said.

"...mission is a failure ... multiple hostiles, repeat we have multiple hostiles inbound ... if anyone can hear this..." The voice died away into static again.

He swore, backed up against a wall, and raised his gun, aiming down the tunnel in front of him. At his side, the demon stood, face pressed against the glass as if it too was trying to look down the tunnel. He spared it one quick glance and then ignored it, eyes forward as he waited for whatever was coming.

And he didn't have to wait long.

The thing that came down the tunnel hadn't bothered to try to disguise itself as human. It was a roiling, seething mass of colours that seemed to be only tenuously held together. As he stared, transfixed, it let out a sound that seemed to reverberate off the walls.

Instinct took over and he fired and kept on firing, until the thing sank to the floor and stopped moving.

He gasped for air, his whole body shaking. Some dim part of him reasoned that he should check that the demon was dead but as he walked towards it, he heard screaming coming from the tunnel. A woman's voice. Ignoring the body, he ran towards the sound.

"Help," she screamed. "Please, somebody help me."

"I'm here," he shouted back. "Where are you?"

There was an awful tearing sound and her cries cut off. Shapes loomed up out of the darkness and he fired into the mass, retreating until he was back at his post.

There was a long moment of terrible silence and then he heard Roth's voice coming over his radio.

"Pete! Pete, are you alright down there?"

"I'm alright. Hostiles have been neutralised."

"What are you talking about? What hostiles?"

He snapped around and stared at the demon. It was laughing, and he realised he could hear it. Coming from his radio. Coming from the tunnels. In the air around him. As he watched, the demon reached out a hand and beckoned.

This story will feature in an upcoming edition of 'Harvey Duckman Presents' to be published in 2022.

The Bracken Hall Witch

Wednesday, February 21st

Dear Diary,

Can you imagine the scandal! A woman taking a coach alone all the way from Measham into Yorkshire. The idea of mother and father having to explain away my absence to the neighbours was almost enough to make me reconsider the whole endeavour, but really I am trying to save their son, after all. And really it was rather fun - at least until we got to those dark, terrible moors. They are exactly as one would expect them to be lonely, desolate places, covered in spiky bracken and dark purple heather and seemingly populated only by ravens. They say the farmers have to guard against them in lambing season, that the ravens will peck out the lambs' eyes if they are allowed to get close enough. It makes me shudder just to think of it.

The coachman wanted to stop for the night at one of the local inns. He said a storm would be gathering and that it would be unsafe for us to be out in the open if we were caught in it. Having no desire to stop at one of the several dingy little inns that he suggested, I paid him an extra guinea to continue on to Bracken Hall. Despite his dire predictions, the weather was fair when we arrived. In fact, the sunset would have been rather spectacular had it not been almost entirely spoiled by the hall itself, looming over the village like some kind of hideous spectre. Why my brother chose to buy this of all places, I will never understand. But then there is much about Alan that I may never understand.

I can only hope that I am not too late to save him from himself.

The coachman at least had the good grace to stay long enough to help me with my bags before he left. Though the speed he was going, I did feel a little sorry for the poor nag that was pulling the coach. Perhaps he was trying to outrun his fictional thunderstorm? More likely there's a woman that his wife has no knowledge of waiting for him in one of those tawdry little inns. Father may think me unworldly, but I know enough to know what men do when they think they will get away with it.

I had hardly lifted my hand to knock on the door (with them having no bell at the front door of this great hall) when who should open it but my brother himself? I was so startled that I almost dropped my bag.

"Rebecca!" he cried out, in a tone most unlike the voice I remember. "What are you doing here?"

I tried to compose myself as I said, "Why, I've come to see you, of course. What else?" but this was no mean feat, given that he had already lifted me off my feet and crushed me in his embrace. This at least is unchanged - he was always given to rather outlandish displays of affection, ever since we were children.

"I'm so happy to see you," he said, when he finally allowed me to stand on solid ground again. "But I wish you had told us you were coming; we have sent the servants home for the night."

"They don't stay here?" I enquired. It did at least explain why the master of the house was answering his own front door.

"No, no, not yet. The servants' quarters are quite uninhabitable at present."

He ran his hand through his hair as he spoke, something I remember him doing only infrequently but always when he was nervous about something. I made no comment on it and let him continue as he told me about how they had prioritised the 'family wing' of the house.

"But you must come and meet Charlotte!" he exclaimed, having presumably exhausted the renovations as a topic of conversation.

I had been hoping to have a little more time with him before he insisted on introducing me to her. The cause of all our woes. And I must not have been quick enough to smother the expression on my face because I saw him frown.

"Sister -" he began, a warning note in his voice.

I placed a hand on his arm. "It is only that I am dusty from the road. I had hoped to be in a better state the first time I met your new bride." I raised my skirts slightly, as though to show him the dust clinging to them.

"Charlotte will not mind," he said.

"Perhaps I mind. Perhaps I am conscious of wanting to make a good first impression."

"If that were the case, you could have done better than to boycott my wedding."

There was a light in his eyes as he spoke that seemed unfamiliar to me, and I will confess to being a little afraid of him in that moment. Can you imagine? Me, afraid of my own brother? It was only for a moment and then I forced a laugh and said, "Well, if you really believe she will not mind, I will gladly come and meet your Charlotte."

"The two of you will be good friends, I know it," he said, as he led me into the house.

We did not have to go far, as it transpires that they have been using the sitting room on an evening while they wait for more renovations to be completed. Alan pushed open the door and there, right in front of me, was the woman herself.

I must admit that she is a good deal more handsome than I had imagined. The way mother speaks of her I had expected some old crone, but she is tall with excellent posture and a face that is troubled only by the finest of fine lines. For a woman nearing forty, her hair seems to have retained its original colour, although it was difficult for me to judge its thickness, bound up as it was.

Yes, Charlotte is a very handsome woman indeed. For a witch.

Thursday, February 22nd

Dear Diary,

I do believe my brother may have lied to me. For all his talk of 'sending the servants home for the night' and assuring me they would be back in the morning, I have yet to see hide or hair of them today. For that matter, I have barely encountered my brother. Every time I leave my room I seem to run into Charlotte, who it appears has been skulking the corridors nearest to the guest room, no doubt in the hopes of talking to me alone. But I know better than to be left alone with a witch, so I always have some excuse on hand - the need to make my toilet for instance, or a pretence that I have forgotten some item for which I must return to my room.

Of course, I shall have to speak to her at dinner. I had hoped that there would be servants present - surely she would not dare to cast her spells in front of witnesses - but it seems likely now that it will just be the three of us. I must be on my guard, for it seems certain that she has already bespelled my brother and she would not hesitate to do the same to me.

Friday, February 23rd

Dear Diary,

I did not get chance to write much yesterday. In writing of mealtimes, it occurred to me that without household help, it is likely that Charlotte prepares the meals. This thought struck me as being one filled with such immediate danger that I threw down my diary and proceeded straight away to the kitchen. I will confess that I was careless in leaving my diary unattended and unhidden and I will be sure not to do so again, however, my fears were well founded. Upon entering the kitchen, I did indeed find Charlotte standing over the stove, in the act of pouring something from a little golden bottle into the pot.

"Ah," she said, as I entered. "There you are. I was beginning to think you would stay in your room all day."

She has one of those faces that I believe she could twist into an expression of absolute innocence if I had caught her standing over a body with a dagger in her hand.

"What are you doing?" I asked.

"Cooking," replied she, with not a trace of guilt in her voice.

"I can see that," I snapped. "What are you adding to the sauce?"

She looked down at the bottle as if she had only just noticed it and then let out a little laugh. She has a child's laugh; high pitched and far too young for someone her age.

"It's just honey," she said. "Some of the herbs grow bitter around here so we use it to sweeten our sauces. It's very good, would you like to try some?"

She held the bottle out towards me, and I fear I may have taken an involuntary step backwards. I do not want to reveal that I know about her, that I know what she is, but really I do not know what worried me more; the honey (which as any sensible person knows is used by witches to sweeten their words) or those bitter herbs she spoke of. What are they? What properties do they hold? And how many of them have I ingested already?

"Perhaps I should help you," I said, ignoring the bottle.

She tried to refuse, telling me that I was a guest and that she would be far too embarrassed to allow someone so above her station to help her with the cooking, but I insisted.

I wonder where her embarrassment was when she seduced my brother.

Saturday, February 24th

Dear Diary,

Perhaps I was premature in announcing that it was worth leaving my diary in plain sight to run down to the kitchen yesterday. When I returned to my room, it appeared to me that it had been moved very slightly from where I left it. But if that is so, then who could have moved it? I was with Charlotte for the whole time. I never let her out of my sight so she would have had no opportunity to go snooping through my belongings. Perhaps after all I am imagining things.

This place certainly lends itself to imaginings. I am not one for flights of fancy, but there is something unsettling about the sheer colour of the air here. If that sounds nonsensical then it is only because it is impossible for me to explain it any other way. Yorkshire in general, and this part in particular, never truly seem to get light. At noon, with the sun at its zenith it is no brighter here than it would be on a gloomy evening at home. And the ravens! They seem to call to one another at all hours of the day and night here. Every time I think I might be about to drop off to sleep, one of them will pierce the silence and then the whole flock of them will start up again. Where are the owls? The nightingales? Where are all the other birds? Could they really have driven them all away?

I was right in my suspicion that I would not see Alan until dinner. He appeared five minutes after Charlotte and I were already seated - and then without so much as a mutter of an apology. I would have passed comment on it, but he did not look at all well. He is pale and drawn, and there are dark circles under his eyes, as if he has not been sleeping properly. He appeared to be stooping, as if he was carrying some great weight on his shoulders, and he fairly dropped into his seat without stopping to greet either one of us.

"Are you quite well?" I asked him.

"Just tired," he replied, with a sigh in his voice.

"Are you not sleeping?" I asked. "Perhaps the cold night air here is not good for you."

I think perhaps he would have allowed me the point, but that damnable woman broke in before he could answer me.

"Alan has been working hard the last few weeks. The former owner left much of the tenant housing in the same state of disrepair as the main house, and he has taken it upon himself to help them rebuild."

Then she had the nerve to look at him the way a woman looks at a man when they are in love. When they are both in love I mean.

I have a terrible headache today. I put it down to my not eating much last night.

Sunday, February 25th

Dear Diary,

I have had the worst day imaginable! I awoke this morning and made my way downstairs only to be met by my brother in the sitting room, wearing what I can only describe as 'workman's clothes'.

"Why are you not dressed for church?" I enquired.

He seemed confused by the question, and even worse, I distinctly heard Charlotte laugh. Oh, she tried to hide it behind her hand, tried to turn it into a polite little cough, but I know what she did.

I turned my back, quite deliberately, on her and spoke to Alan only. I implored him to come to church with me and I reminded him of the danger to his immortal soul should he turn his back on God. It took more persuading than I would have thought possible, but he did eventually agree to accompany me. Even then, I am sure I saw him glance at Charlotte, as though he was asking for her permission. Or perhaps, for her forgiveness.

Charlotte elected to remain at home, and since her immortal soul - if she even possesses such a thing - is no concern of mine, I did not exert any pressure on her to do otherwise. If anything, I was glad to have some time alone with Alan. I was hopeful that I might be able to talk some sense into him once we were away from her influence. However, this proved to be more difficult than I had anticipated. The walk to the church is not a long one but, with no time to lose, I began to bring up their rather hasty arrangement almost as soon as we were out of earshot of the house. Of her, I mean. The walls may have ears but not literally, not even in Yorkshire. Truth be told, the conversation was something of a disaster. Alan seems to be distracted by the most inane things; interrupting me every few moments to point out this or that flower, or tree. As if we did not have flowers or trees at home! I finally reached up and took him by the shoulders, turning him towards me that he might see how serious I am, but I had no sooner forced him to look at me than a great wind sprang up, seemingly out of nowhere. It almost ripped my bonnet from my head and it forced us to make haste to the church for shelter of the physical as well as the metaphysical variety.

What could it be but a hex? Gale force winds do not appear without warning.

I am afraid that I was too angry to pay much attention to the sermon. Perhaps if I had spent less time thinking about Charlotte and more time paying attention to my surroundings, I would have noticed what my brother was doing. In fact, what I actually noticed was the way the churchgoers were staring. At first I thought they were staring at me, but when I turned to Alan to comment on their rudeness, I realised that he had fallen fast asleep. Try as I might, I was unable to wake him until after the service had finished. That vile woman! I almost have to admire the cleverness of her - she was unable to prevent me from taking him to the church, so she made sure that he did not hear a word of the sermon. She is a cunning foe indeed.

My time here is running out. Any day now, mother and father will realise where I am and send for me. Once that happens, Charlotte will use it as an excuse to send me home and I will have no choice but to leave Alan alone with her again.

I have terrible hunger pangs, but I dare not eat anything that I have not cooked myself. In any other circumstances I would feel terribly rude refusing Charlotte's hospitality in this manner, but this may be a matter of life and death.

Tuesday, February 26th

Dear Diary,

I felt too weak to bother writing yesterday but I cannot let the day pass without reporting what has happened. Finally, after almost a week in this accursed place, I have come across some evidence of Charlotte's evil nature. Irrefutable evidence, in fact.

It occurred to me last night that Charlotte is watching me every bit as much as I am watching her. Neither one of us can go anywhere in this place (our private chambers excepted, of course) without the other one being aware of everything we are doing. And as Charlotte never leaves the house, I have had no opportunity to look for anything that might incriminate her.

But that is only in the daytime. And the more I thought about it, the more I realised that if I want to look around this place, it cannot be in daylight. There were risks, of course. After all, the witch is a creature of darkness and surely her power will be stronger then. But, having decided that needs must, I screwed up my courage and crept out of my room as soon as the house descended into silence.

The first thing that struck me as I crept downstairs was the smell. The whole house smelt overpoweringly of white lilies. Although I do not remember seeing any lilies earlier, it appears that while I slept great bouquets of them have been placed in the hallways, the sitting room and the little room that I assume Alan is using as his study. I have never known my brother to have any great fondness for flowers so this must be her doing. I do not know whether lilies have any great significance in witchcraft (although I myself have always associated them with death) so I shall pass on to the next piece of information.

After seeing Charlotte pour the honey into the sauce, I felt that the kitchen would be the logical place to start my explorations. It is a large room that in any other home would no doubt be 'airy' but in this place it is crammed with boxes and jars of strange substances. In one cupboard I found what I can only describe as 'potions' poured into small glass bottles and sealed with wax. They have no writing on the labels (or at least none that I could read) but I wonder whether they might have been colour coded in some way? The more dangerous concoctions in the darker hued bottles, for instance? With no way to discern what was inside the bottles, I returned them to the cupboard, being careful to replace them exactly where I found them, and continued on my way.

It was at this point that I began to feel as though I might not be alone. I felt a strange sensation, like breath on the back of my neck, but when I turned there was no one there. Back in the hall, I passed a mirror and for a second I thought that I saw someone standing behind me. I almost cried out, but I managed to stop myself just in time. There was no one there, of course. Candlelight will play strange tricks with a person's nerves - especially if that person happens to be tired, hungry and more than a little overwrought.

As silly as I felt about the whole mirror incident, it turned out to be a good thing. As I glanced about me to make sure that I really was alone, something caught my eye, illuminated as it was by my candle. There, tucked into a crevice in the wall was a small doll. I would never have noticed it, but for the button eyes which seemed to flash in the little light. It was a tiny figure, unmistakably female as denoted by the longish hair and crude dress.

It can only be one thing. A poppet. A poppet of me.

Wednesday, February 27th

Dear Diary,

What is a person to do when she finds a poppet of oneself? I could hardly burn it or bury it - who knows what that would do to me. In the end I decided that the safest course of action was to take it with me and hide it amongst my possessions until I can find some way to safely rid myself of the evil thing. At least that way Charlotte will be unable to use it against me.

I am so afraid. But I have found at least one person, perhaps the only person, to whom I can confide my fears. After the events of the previous night, I needed to get away from Bracken Hall, to go out into what passes for sunshine in these parts and try to clear my head. It seemed that the smell of the lilies had followed me even into my dreams and were trailing behind me like a ghost.

The only place that I knew that I would feel truly safe is the little church, for surely the witch's power must be greatly diminished there. I had intended only to pray for guidance but as I knelt on the stones, I was disturbed by a movement at the front of the building, near the altar. At first I was so frightened that I almost ran from the church, but I was stopped by a familiar, kindly voice and I recognised the figure, not as some hideous conjuration, but as the priest whose sermon my brother had so rudely slept through several days ago. Of course, I attempted to apologise for his behaviour, but he waved away my words as though they were so much chaff in the air. He asked me whether I would like to take confession and there was something searching in his eyes as he spoke to me, something that told me he knew at least some of what was going on at the hall. I am very much afraid that I broke down and cried on his shoulder as I told him all that I knew, all that I had discovered in the last few days.

His name is Father Simon. He has been the priest here at St Mary's church for the last four years and he is well aware of some of the stranger comings and goings at Bracken Hall. I told him of the necessity of rescuing my brother from the witch and he agreed that this must be my sacred mission, that my brother's soul is imperilled should I fail.

He has given me a silver cross to wear, which he took from around his own neck, blessing it and kissing it before he draped it around my own. He has also given me a small vial of holy water which he told me that I must hide about my person when I confront Charlotte. And I must confront her - I must cast her away, bargain with her for my brother's safety, do whatever I must to save him from her. To save him from himself.

Father Simon has been a great comfort to me. He will hold the church in readiness for me should my brother and I need a sanctuary once we escape from Bracken Hall – and from the witch who resides within it.

Thursday, February 28th

Dear Diary,

I believe that Charlotte grows in power every day. The more I look upon her, the less human she seems. Indeed, now she strikes me as more of a wild thing that has been stuffed into civilised clothing than a human woman. Each day, her hair seems to uncoil itself a little more, her eyes seem to glow a little brighter, her skin seems a little paler. There is a look in her eyes that I could best describe as 'hungry', as if she would devour us all if she could. Perhaps she can.

Today the moment I most feared has arrived. A messenger came to the house with a letter from mother and father. If I had only managed to intercept it, I might have bought myself a few more precious days, but unfortunately it was addressed to Alan, and he was the one to open it.

I confess, I felt some of sympathy for him when he brandished it at me; there must have been a moment before he read it when he recognised our father's handwriting, when he may have thought that he had been forgiven. Certainly, that would go some way to explaining the rage in his eyes when he told me that my time here is over, that he would send me away as soon as he could arrange appropriate transport for me.

I begged him to come with me, I even went so far as to cite the unsuitability of a woman travelling such a long way on her own, but he refused me, telling me that since I had come here alone I should not object to being asked to return home alone. Charlotte, of course, said nothing.

My time here is short now, I may only have a matter of days. I must do as Father Simon suggested and confront the witch. Perhaps there is some way for me to convince her to renounce her hold on my brother. I carry the cross on my person at all times now. It brings me some comfort.

Saturday, February 29th

Dear Diary,

I did it! I confronted the witch. I waited until Alan was out visiting the tenants and then I invited her to come for a picnic with me. Of course, she refused to leave the grounds (I really believe that her power is somehow tied to this place) but at least we were outside the house where people could hear me if I had begun to scream. In any case, I was wearing the silver cross and vial of holy water that Father Simon gave me, and I felt a great deal safer than I have done since my arrival here. All the same I waited until she had a mouthful of food before I spoke. Surely the witch cannot curse me if she cannot speak.

"I know what you are," I told her.

She raised an eyebrow and continued to chew, albeit a little faster than before.

"Everyone told me what you were when you convinced my brother to marry you. Why else would a twenty-six-year-old man, the heir to a fortune no less, agree to marry a forty-year-old widow with no money and no social standing. Even so I hardly believed it until I came here and saw it for myself. Your poppets. Your potions. I know what you are. Witch."

She laughed. She actually laughed at me! And not that silly high-pitched giggle either but a full, throaty laugh, the laugh of an adult woman. And when she had finished laughing she looked me full in the face and claimed that the spells and poppets were not hers at all, that she had cast no spell over my brother.

That he was the one who had cast the spell on her.

"Why do you think I cannot leave this place?" she asked me. "It is because your brother will not allow it."

My brother. My kind, generous brother who would never have left us had this harridan not bewitched him until he was out of his right mind. It was my turn to laugh.

"I know exactly why you cannot leave here, hag," I told her. "You draw your power from this place somehow. That is why it never gets light here, why the ravens never leave."

There was something strange on her face as I spoke, something I could not quite place. Suddenly she leaned forward, and made a grab for my arm. I threw myself back, out of her reach.

"You will not have him," I told her. "I will take him with me when I leave. Away from this place. Away from you."

I made good my escape before she had time to reach out for me again. I headed quickly out of the grounds and towards the church. When I looked back, she was standing at the gate watching me. I could smell the storm gathering in the air and I knew that I must speak to Father Simon, I must ask him to send a messenger to Bracken Hall, to intercept my brother before he has time to speak to her.

Update – Feb. 29th

I am sitting in the church now. Father Simon has sent his messenger and he assures me that my brother will be here with me before nightfall. If I can only speak to him, away from her influence, I know that I can convince him to see sense.

In a moment I will put down my diary and I will pray for the strength to do what I must. I need to pray, but I need to make a record of everything that has happened here too. There must be a record. Charlotte must be held accountable. Tonight, I will leave, with my brother, or not at all.

Wednesday, March 14th

Dear Diary,

Tonight will be my first night in my own bed in almost three weeks. I have had a lovely time with the cousins in Bath, although the way mother complained about my absence is terribly strange, given that she was the one who suggested it in the first place!

I believe that she might have been snooping through my diary. Several pages appear to have been torn out, which I certainly would not have done. I tried to make out the entries on the scraps of paper that have been left at the heart of the book but the only word I could make out was 'Alan'.

I wish I could remember writing the entries that have vanished, if only to solve the mystery of who on earth this 'Alan' could be.

Acknowledgements

Thank you to Mum and Dad, Anne, Mike, Elliott and Marcus, Paula, Debs, David, Sophie and Megs, Jo, Craig and Laura for your continued enthusiasm and support.

Thanks to Frankie at 3Moon for publishing 'The Turning' and to all at 'Harvey Duckman Presents' for publishing 'A Rum Affair', 'By Firelight' and 'Gosfeld'.

Thank you most of all to John.

About the Author

Amy Wilson is a writer and editor from Teesside, in the North of England. She has written stories for the 'Harvey Duckman Presents' series of anthologies in the UK and for 3Moon Magazine and the 'From One Line' anthologies in the US, as well as contributing stories to the 'No Sleep' podcast and to National Flash Fiction Day's 'Flash Flood' event.

She was nominated for an award for her microfiction story, 'The Colour of Darkness' in summer 2021.

Her first book, a collection of microfiction entitled 'Micro Moods', was published in November 2021. Her novel, 'Grave Tidings' is due for publication in 2023.

You can find out more about Amy by going to www.amywilson.co.uk or by following her @WritesAmy on Instagram and Twitter.

Coming Soon - Grave Tidings

The following is an excerpt from the novel, 'Grave Tidings', due for publication in 2023.

It was not a dark and stormy night.

Perhaps it ought to have been for what they were doing, but the sun hung obstinately in the sky - as though refusing to hide its face behind one of the white, fluffy clouds that periodically drifted by - and she could spare no more time.

Three days he had been in the grave. Three days almost to the hour and if she was ever going to retrieve him from his resting place then it would have to be now. She gathered her courage as she stared down at the soft mound of recently disturbed earth that was the only thing that marked out the grave. There had not been either the money or the time for a headstone; his family had not had the money and she had not had the time to prepare one. By the time she learned of his untimely demise (from his sister, who had answered her insistent questioning with great reluctance on her part) his body was more than forty-eight hours cold. Almost too late.

She would never have forgiven herself if she had been too late, and as for what she would have done to his sisters, well that didn't bear thinking about.

The cemetery was full of people milling about. Mostly, she guessed, those who were using one of the few available green spaces in the city as a kind of makeshift park in the absence of being able to afford to go to an actual park. For the third time in as many minutes she cursed the nice weather and the brightness of the day. Still, it couldn't be helped. People died at lunchtime and therefore she would just have to do her work now, inconvenience be damned.

"Hurry," she urged Brodie.

He responded with a noncommittal grunt and straightened, pressing one hand into his lower back in the silent protest of manual workers everywhere.

"Double if he's out in the next," she squinted at the sun, "five minutes."

His eyes widened and he bent to his task, throwing forkfuls of mud carelessly over his shoulder as he worked.

Her fingers itched to grab a spade and join him. The work could only have gone faster with two of them at it, but if the sight of a man digging in a cemetery while a woman stood in widows' weeds and watched him was strange enough, the sight of that woman climbing into the grave and digging through the contents would definitely have drawn attention of the sort that she couldn't afford right now. She cast her eyes about her from beneath the safety of her veil and was pleased to see that no one was paying them much heed. Common decency should have dictated that no one stop and stare at what appeared to be a grieving woman, standing out against the crowds of sun-worshippers, but as she was very well aware, common decency was not always enough to provide protection.

After what seemed an age (but judging by the smug expression on Brodie's face could not have been more than a couple of minutes) she heard his fork hit something solid. He dropped the fork, grabbed the shovel, and started scraping loose soil from the top of the coffin.

Not quite six feet, she noted silently to herself. Cheapskates.

Brodie had brought along a crowbar to prise the lid off the coffin, but once it was uncovered he had only to run the shovel along the outer edge and then pull against it and the lid dislodged.

She found that she was holding her breath as Brodie moved the lid to one side. The first thing she noticed was the smell. She had been preparing herself for the sickly tang of embalmers fluid, but there was nothing beyond the loamy scent of fresh cut earth. A kind of rage rose up in her chest (they didn't even pay to have him embalmed! They would have let his corpse rot away to nothing!) before she remembered that it suited her purposes better if she did not have to drain his body of that poison. She took a moment to look down at his face. They had at least put coins over his eyes – a ridiculous superstition of course, but something that passed for respect around here – and beneath them, his face was calm and pallid. The old truism that he could almost have been sleeping did not hold here; there was a certain something missing from the man she had known, a slackness in his face that had been absent in life. But there was still enough of him that she could restore what had been.

"Pick him up," she ordered.

Brodie had to climb into the hole, straddling the coffin to raise him onto his shoulders. As he did so she could see the bruises creeping up his hands and arms where the blood had pooled, and she thought again of the embalmer.

Blood is better, she reminded herself, gritting her teeth to keep from cursing.

With what she could only assume was the mark of a professional grave robber, Brodie climbed easily out of the hole, balancing the corpse on one shoulder.

"'Ere," said a voice, too close for comfort.

"He's my husband," she said, without turning.

"That don't mean -" the voice said, but she had no intention of staying around for long enough to hear out the rest of the argument.

Brodie being similarly disinclined to wait around, the two of them set off back towards the coach. She moved with a naturally long stride that was somewhat hampered by her skirts and Brodie moved with a naturally long stride that was somewhat hampered by the dead man on his shoulder. Shouts rose up around them as they passed through the cemetery - and one more than one occasion she heard a loud shriek. Neither of them slowed their pace until they reached the coach, and if the driver was surprised to see his mistress return with an infamous grave robber and a dead man, then he knew better than to say anything about it.

He waited until she was seated, and the corpse was safely stowed on the floor of the coach, before urging the horses into a smart trot that carried them away from the rapidly growing crowd.

Micro Moods - Out Now

'A masterclass of short form writing'

'Unique and brilliant'

'Small but beautifully crafted'

'A wonderful read'

Whether you want to read about the value of memories in 'A Penny for your Thoughts', a long-awaited vengeance in 'The Debt' or even about an ogre with a love of stand-up comedy in 'A Captive Audience', there's sure to be something to fit your mood!

Available now, via Amazon.

Printed in Great Britain
by Amazon

78308534R00105